CW00802696

Deal with Mr. Cruel

An agreement with consequences

You are mine 2

Rebecca Baker

Copyright 2023
Rebecca Baker
All rights reserved

Sign up for my newsletter and receive a free romance novel:
https://dl.bookfunnel.com/oe2w1m9zxx

Chapter 1

Jonas

The lights of the city glimmered, casting reflections on the window. Jonas pressed his forehead against the cool glass and looked out over the cityscape. His breath left foggy prints, leaving just as quickly as they appeared.

He could faintly hear the party from downstairs. The drinks clinking. The laughter. The chatter. Usually, these sounds would entice him, but tonight he was tired. A hint of guilt crept in as he thought about his secretary, Wendy, who had been on the phone for weeks, hiring vendors and finalizing the guest list. "It's a big deal, boss," she had said, even though he was hesitant about a party.

His first year heading up his father's company had flown by. Despite his many accomplishments, Jonas still had impostor's syndrome. Even so, this was where he was meant to be. It was where he *had* to be if he wanted to become the most successful man in Boston. He knew he had a lot left to prove.

Jonas stood with his thoughts for a moment before he let out a sigh and pushed away from the glass. He glanced at his watch. It was just after seven o'clock. The night was still young. And so was he. Hell, he wasn't even forty yet. He should go down to the party, but Jonas didn't want anyone suggesting he was getting old, and he probably would punch anyone who did. He shook his head to wake up. Time to be the boss.

After straightening the papers on his desk, he grabbed his phone and slid it into his pants pocket. With a glance at his reflection in the window, Jonas smoothed his dark hair back with his hands. He tightened his tie and slid a jacket over his shoulders. Happy with what he saw, he headed out of his office.

The hall was empty as he made his way toward the elevators. Everyone had clocked out already and was down at the party. Jonas pressed the button and leaned against the wall, waiting for one to open. Every now and then in the silence, he could still hear his father barking orders or making snide comments under his breath. The contrast was so different, but the underlying tone was the same. His father had been feared by his employees, which was probably why the company was so successful. Jonas had also feared his father until the feelings became blurry and turned to hate.

The ding of the elevator broke Jonas from his thoughts, and he stood from the wall as the elevator doors slid open. Unsurprisingly, it was empty. He hit the button for the second floor and rode down to the faint sound of a piano drifting from the speakers. Soon, the doors opened, and loud music came pouring in, invading the quiet. Jonas stepped out of the elevator and stood back, watching the party. It was massive. He wondered if this was a celebration for him or for one year of being without the big, bad boss. Plastering a smile on his face and stepping out of the elevator, Jonas let the thought go.

Looking around, he saw that Wendy really had invited everyone. All the bigwigs in the city. The entire Major League team. His family. She even got Nate Brockton to come, who was ordering drinks at the bar with a long-haired brunette hanging on him like silk. Jonas had been desperately trying to secure a deal with him ever since he took over the company.

Nate headed one of the largest sporting apparel companies on the east coast. Jonas had been wanting to expand the company to include apparel for years, but his father always stood firm in his opposing opinion. He never had listened to Jonas's ideas. His father was headstrong—although some would say he had his head far up his ass.

After many meetings, Jonas had come to realize that Nate didn't make a deal with just anybody. They had to work for it, which made securing the deal that much more appealing. Jonas straightened his jacket and started heading toward the bar to schmooze with his future potential business partner.

But then he saw her.

Mae leaned against the back wall, holding a glass of champagne. She was talking to her brother, Nico, and let out a laugh that lit up her entire face. Almost as though she sensed him, Mae glanced up at Jonas across the room and closed her mouth into a tight-lipped smile. She gave a small nod and lifted her glass before taking a sip of champagne. Then her attention went back to her brother. Such a small gesture made Jonas feel as if his feet were cemented in place, and his gaze remained on her. Mae wore a red dress that hugged her curves like it was clinging to her for dear life. Her blonde hair was pulled back loosely, and a few tendrils escaped and brushed against her face as she talked.

Mae seemed enthralled by what Nico was saying, which wasn't surprising with how much she cared for her baby brother. Jonas couldn't help but feel a tinge of jealousy. Mae had always been protective of Nico, and she had good reason to be, as he was one of the wilder guys on the team. Nico had just made it to the big leagues and it seemed to go to his head. He was always getting in some sort of trouble she had to navigate him out of. Jonas often had to crack down on him, which Nico resented him for. If only Mae didn't baby him so much, then maybe he would grow up. But, she'd taken on the motherly role when they lost both of their parents unexpectedly.

"She looks good," a voice said, breaking Jonas from his stare.

Jonas cleared his throat. "Hmm?" he asked innocently, glancing at Chad, who stood holding out a glass of whiskey and ice.

"Thank you," Jonas said, accepting the glass and taking a sip. He reluctantly turned his back to Mae and looked around at the party. Silver streamers hung from the ceiling, and a disco ball slowly spun in the center of the room, casting light in a thousand different directions. A large ice sculpture of a baseball stood tall next to the bar.

"Wendy really went all out," he said.

"Of course she did. You did it! You successfully took over the business from your father. The owner from hell."

Jonas let out a chuckle and shook his head, looking down at his glass.

"In all seriousness, you've really taken the company to the next level. We've signed more athletes and advertised at more games than ever before. We needed someone fresh and young-ish," Chad said with a wink.

"Watch yourself. I'm still your boss," Jonas replied, raising an eyebrow.

"You're hers now too," Chad said, nodding toward Mae.

"We are strictly professional."

"Sure, you are."

Jonas remained silent, swirling his glass of whiskey as the ice clinked against the sides.

"What's the deal with you two, anyway?" Chad asked.

"That's ancient history."

Chad nodded and took the last swig from his drink. "I'm all out," he said before heading to the bar.

Jonas watched him walk away before letting out a deep breath. He hated how well Chad knew him and hoped he wasn't as transparent to the rest of his employees. An office fling wouldn't look professional. He couldn't risk losing the respect he had built over the past year. Still, he couldn't help thinking about Mae.

She rarely spoke to him and was sure to never be alone with him. Mae was always professional, but there was a coldness only he could feel. No one else seemed to notice. Most days, her curt attitude pissed him off, but on rare days, he felt a tinge of longing. Only once had he had the courage to set things right, but he hung up before he dialed the last number of her office extension. Several other times, he fantasized about calling her into his office to do more than talk.

Both ideas were impossible. He'd lost his chance years ago. He'd had her. Her mind, her heart, her body. She had really listened to him when he was in the throes with his father. Mae encouraged him and quietly cheered him on in the office. Jonas still remembered his fingers tangled in her hair, her lips parted against his, and her fingers trailing his chest. There were times he knew she wanted to tell him her feelings, but he never let her get that close.

The spark between them was sudden and strong, and then he'd extinguished it. He couldn't let his feelings get away from him in an office romance. A distraction. A roadblock to success. These were all things he told himself as the weight of what Mae really meant to him started closing in. What they had was real, and it scared him.

So, Jonas had ended it. His sudden coldness had taken Mae by surprise. She didn't say much, but he saw the sad understanding in her eyes. He was wrong, but his pride couldn't take the scrutinizing eyes of his father, who didn't believe in silly things like love. Jonas threw himself into his job and worked his way up the company. He convinced himself he didn't need a woman when there was so much to accomplish. Deep down, Jonas didn't want to be like his father, who had lost his mother due to his coldness, but it was the only way he knew.

"What do you think?" Wendy asked, her voice bringing him back to the present.

He looked at his secretary, who stood expectantly waiting for his response.

"You've really outdone yourself. Truly."

"Everyone who is anyone is here," she said, beaming.

"I can see. You even got Nate here."

"It wasn't easy. It looks like his girlfriend has pried herself away from him. Now's your chance."

Jonas looked toward the bar and nodded. He took the last sip of his whiskey and set his glass down on a nearby table.

"You've got this, boss!" Wendy whispered after him.

He did have this. He was one of the youngest CEOs in Boston. The city's entire beloved sports team was in this room to celebrate him. He had a business proposal that was hard to refuse and would make him millions. Also, he could have—almost - any woman he wanted. In fact, he would go out to his favorite bar after this and take someone home.

Jonas started feeling like himself again as he made his way across the room. He smiled confidently as he passed employees who nodded and raised their glasses to him. A few patted his back. Despite the boost in confidence, he could still feel Mae. It annoyed him how constantly aware of her he was.

And how could he not be aware of her now? Her red dress was striking and made her stand out from the crowd of suits and ties. She stood directly in his path to the bar where Nate was scrolling through his phone. Jonas politely excused himself as he pushed gently through the crowd. As he got closer to her, his heart rate quickened. Mae's back was turned toward him, and he sucked in a quiet breath as he brushed past her. The familiar scent of vanilla and lavender wafted up at him. He pushed away the memories that came crashing in.

From the corner of his eye, he watched her turn her head slightly and felt her gaze on him as he continued. The question of "what if" briefly entered his mind, and then he found himself face-to-face with Nate. Jonas composed himself. He wouldn't let her get to him again. Not now. Not ever.

He cleared his throat. "Nate. Thank you for coming."

Chapter 2

Mae

Pulling at her dress and willing it to be longer, Mae tried paying attention to her brother talk about his latest night out. She wondered why she had worn such a sexy dress to an office party, but deep down, she knew it was for Jonas. This whole party was for him, and here she was laughing a little too loud at her brother's antics, trying to look comfortable. Trying to look like she was unbothered. Normally, Nico's stories of drunken nights at parties and jumping off roofs into the pool would put her into mama-bear mode, but tonight, she was distracted. Distracted by Jonas in his navy suit, the chatter surrounding him, and this damn dress that kept riding up.

She almost hadn't come. Spending an evening celebrating a man who broke her heart, although she'd never admit it, didn't sound all that appealing. Nico's lack of a date swayed her, though. She would much rather be on her brother's arm than some girl who was into him for the wrong reasons. He was a conquest to many. A professional baseball player they could cross off their list, or worse, try to cling to for the fame and fortune.

Maybe she was too protective, although Nico would say she was harsh. He recently stopped introducing Mae to anyone new because she was too critical. She had to be. She was his big sister, and he didn't have anyone else.

Their parents had passed away unexpectedly in a car accident ten years ago. She still remembered the red and blue lights flickering through the sheer curtains of the living room. The knock on the door. The policemen removing their hats and holding them in their hands. She had to steady herself against the doorframe. She had wanted to scream, but she held it in, and the loudness vibrated between the walls in her head.

At nineteen, Mae became her brother's legal guardian. In their will, their parents had left them the house. It felt comforting to stay in the only place they knew, but it also felt sad because pieces were missing. It took every bit of strength for Mae to carry on. If she didn't keep it together, who would? Not Nico. He was only fourteen and smack dab in the middle of adolescence. He didn't handle their parents' deaths well. The loss turned him upside down.

Mae had to keep it together for the both of them. During the day, she made sure Nico got to school on time, did his studies, went to baseball practice, and she cheered him on at every game. At night, she crumbled. She lay in bed, trying to sleep between her quiet sobs.

Through the years, they'd leaned on each other. Once Nico graduated from high school, he went to a state school on a baseball scholarship. He persuaded Mae to get her bachelor's degree alongside him. She took online courses and earned her degree in sports marketing. While this wasn't exactly her dream, she did what she could to stay close to her brother. After they graduated, she got a job in the sports business, and Nico made it to the Major Leagues. She still couldn't believe they had made it out of such a dark period of their lives.

Looking at her brother, she was proud of him. She was proud of herself. Mae smiled at him sentimentally and took a sip of champagne.

"What?" Nico asked, taking a pause in his story and raising an eyebrow.

"Nothing," Mae said with a shrug. "I guess I'm just proud of you."

"For jumping from three stories up? How much champagne have you had?"

She gave him a playful shove. "No! Don't ever do that again. I mean *this*." She motioned toward the party with her hands. "You made it," she said.

"I couldn't have done it without you," he said softly.

"They'd be proud of you too."

"You think?" he asked, a hint of sadness in his voice.

"I know," she said reassuringly.

"You're a pretty good date, sis."

"Best one you've had in years," she said with a wink.

"I'm going to go grab some hors d'oeuvres. Do you want anything?" Nico asked, pointing his thumb at the buffet table.

"Grab me some of those cheese ball things," she said. "I'll get us some more champagne."

The one good thing about this party was the food. The free booze wasn't too bad either. Wendy always chose the best caterers for their events. She had also spared no expense with this party.

Mae made her way to the bar and ordered two glasses of champagne. She chatted with a few of the players at the bar. They had all come to be like brothers to her. There was a time they may have flirted with her, but Nico put an end to that quickly. Now they were just one big family. The previous owner had loved Nico, almost to a fault by being too lenient with him. Now that Jonas was in charge, that all changed. Honestly, everything had changed.

Mae thought back to the night when Jonas had ended things between them. They lay in his bed, tangled in the sheets with a bucket of champagne between them, sipping straight from the bottle. Jonas had just received a promotion that he'd been working hard toward. He worked harder than anyone she knew. Most fathers would go a little easy on their children. Maybe show some favoritism. But not Jonas's. If anything, he made it harder.

Mae knew how important it was for Jonas to prove himself to his father. His father was hated in the office. He was a scrooge, but she had a soft spot for him because of how supportive he was of Nico. She often wondered if Jonas was jealous of their relationship.

"I finally did it," Jonas had said in disbelief. He ran his fingers softly through her hair. She loved when he played with her hair. It was one of the things that comforted her the most.

Mae nuzzled against his chest. "I knew you'd get it. All those hours you've put in and the new clients you've won over. You deserve it. Now give me some of that champagne."

He let out a little laugh and handed her the bottle. She propped herself up on her elbow to take a swig. She looked up at him as the bubbles ran down her throat.

"What's next, Mr. Vice President?" she said playfully, running her finger up his chest.

He looked at her and smiled. She'd never forget how sad a smile could look.

"What is it?" she asked, concerned.

"We can't keep seeing each other, Mae," he said, putting his hand gently against her face. "You know that, right?"

She remained silent. Stunned.

This thing between them was only a few months in, but it had hit her hard and fast. Deep down, she knew an office romance would complicate things, which was why they kept it a secret. Eventually, if things became serious enough, she'd thought they could go public. Mae wanted nothing more than to be on his arm, not cooped up inside his place. She thought Jonas felt the same or would in time.

Jonas continued, "This new position is huge. I need to take it seriously. If my father found out I was having a fling with an employee…"

"A fling?" she said, pulling back. Mae's eyes stung with tears, but she blinked them back.

"You know what I mean."

"Actually, I don't."

He was silent for a moment. "I'm sorry, Mae."

Her sadness suddenly turned to anger. She wrapped herself in sheets and stood up from the bed.

"So, you invited me over for—whatever *this* was, just to break things off?" she asked, gesturing to the bed and feeling her cheeks flush.

"I wanted a chance to explain everything."

Mae let out a laugh. "Well, you should have done that before you took my clothes off," she said, frantically gathering her dress and panties from the floor. She started toward the bathroom. "You know what? You're just like him."

"Who?"

"The man everyone hates."

She slammed the bathroom door, but not before seeing the hurt flash in his eyes.

Just then, the bartender placed two bubbling champagne flutes onto the countertop, bringing her out of her memories and back to the party.

"Thank you," Mae said softly as she left a few dollars in the tip jar.

She walked carefully through the crowd to find Nico. Everyone's glasses started clinking. In the front of the room, Jonas was being pushed forward as everyone circled him. He had his hands in his pockets, and he shrugged awkwardly. Even awkward, he was still annoyingly handsome. Dark hair fell in his face as he laughed uncomfortably. For being a big CEO, he sure didn't like public speaking. She couldn't help but smile as he squirmed. For a brief moment, she let her real feelings surface.

Just then, he looked up and his eyes caught hers. She felt her cheeks flush. His eyes were a striking green. Somehow, at this crowded party, she felt like she was the only one in the room. Fearing he could see right through her, she tore her eyes away and walked in the opposite direction. She couldn't stay here any longer. She had to get out of here. Mae spotted Nico and bore toward him.

"Whoa, sis. What's up?" he asked, eyeing her.

"Nothing. I'm just tired," she said, handing him his champagne.

He checked his watch. "Uh. It's just after eight," he said, raising an eyebrow.

"I know. It's been a long day."

"Okay," Nico said hesitantly.

"I'm fine, I'm fine." She waved him away. "You don't have to come home with me. I'll get a cab. You go have fun," Mae said reassuringly. She knew the other players had plans to go out to bars after this. While Nico lived with her, she didn't want him to feel babied. At least not all the time. In fact, it was probably time he started looking for his own place. Although, she wasn't sure if she was ready to let him go just yet.

"Are you sure? It looks like the boss man is about to make a speech," he said, nodding toward the front of the room.

"I'm sure." She hugged Nico quickly and placed her unfinished glass of champagne on a nearby table. She stepped outside just as everyone started chanting, "Speech! Speech! Speech!"

Outside in the cool air, she took in a deep breath. Away from Jonas, she could relax again. What was it about tonight? Usually, she was fine working in the same office. Well, not fine, but fine enough. She kept her distance and kept their communication typed out between their inboxes. Some days, when she felt that pang in her heart, she felt tempted to look for another job. But she wanted to be close to Nico so she could keep an eye on him. Or maybe it was she wanted to be close to Jonas, too.

Mae shook her head and held her hand out for a cab. Almost immediately, one pulled up to the curb. She opened the door and gave the driver her address. The car slowly pulled away as she glanced up at the building where she worked. Leaning her head against the window, she let out a sigh. She couldn't wait to get home, change into an oversized shirt, and crash on the couch.

"Did you have a good night, miss?" the driver asked, looking at her in the rearview mirror.

Mae nodded. She had gone and showed her face and bared more than she intended in this red dress. Instead of bailing, she went to a party for the man she used to love. She never told him. It was probably better that way.

Chapter 3

Jonas

Jonas stood at the bar pretending to listen to a bubbly redhead who kept mixing up football terminology with baseball, trying to sound like she actually watched the sport. He politely nodded and looked around the bar for anyone to come save him. He spotted Nico talking with a few players and wondered where Mae was. He was kind of annoyed with her for leaving tonight's party so quickly, and the blur of her red dress walking out the door kept playing repeatedly in his mind.

He had come out to the bars to try and distract himself. Now he was stuck listening to this girl talk about how she watched the touchdown in the ninth inning. He couldn't help but let out a laugh under his breath. She raised an eyebrow at him questioningly. He cleared his throat and let her continue. Jonas was used to women like this. Pretending they cared about the sport of baseball, trying to impress him. He knew they weren't really interested in *him*. They were interested in who he was or who he could connect them with. That's why nothing serious ever came out of nights like this, and that's exactly how he wanted it.

He spotted Chad across the bar and gave him a look that could only be determined as a cry for help. Chad nodded knowingly, finished his drink, and walked over to Jonas. He was one of the vets on the team, and they had formed a solid friendship over the years. Despite being the oldest on the team, Chad could still hold his own with the team, on and off the field.

"Hey, boss. Sorry to interrupt, but I have someone I need you to meet."

The redhead shot Chad a look, and then softened when she realized who he was. Her interest was even more piqued. "Aren't you—?"

Before she could finish, Chad cut her off. "It's business, darling."

Jonas looked at her with as much regret as he could muster up, while internally breathing a sigh of relief.

"Duty calls," Jonas said with a little salute, before turning to walk away.

"But you didn't get my number," she called after him as they walked away.

"Thanks, man," he said, patting Chad on the back.

"I know a cry for help when I see one. Although…she was pretty hot. What gives?" Chad asked, looking back over his shoulder.

"You should go back and talk to her. You'll see. She's convinced a baseball is brown with laces."

Chad let out a laugh. "That bad, huh?"

"You have no idea."

Chad led Jonas to the other side of the bar where most of the team was standing around playing drinking games at a large high-top. They all stood a little straighter when Jonas approached.

"At ease, gentlemen," Jonas said.

They gave an uneasy laugh.

"Loosen up, boys," Chad said, slapping two players on the back. "Let's let the boss join in."

The team made room for Jonas to sidle up to the table.

"Bartender! Another beer!" Chad shouted. The bartender nodded. She was used to this. The team frequented the place often. Soon, Jonas had a drink in hand and was playing quarters. The rest of the bar patrons looked on at their rowdy but beloved team and its owner.

"Oyyyy!" Nico shouted, slapping his hands on the table. He had made his quarter in the cup. He picked up the glass full of beer and started debating who he would give it to. He locked eyes with Jonas and smiled mischievously. "Here you go, boss." He slid the beer toward Jonas.

Jonas held his hands up in protest, but the team started chanting, "Chug it! Chug it! Chug it!"

He shook his head and put the glass to his lips. This was ridiculous, but he was having fun. He drank the beer quickly and slammed the glass on the table as the team cheered.

"So, this was the very important business you had to attend to?" A voice interrupted their game. Jonas looked up and saw the redhead he had narrowly escaped earlier. He gave her a shrug and an apologetic smile.

"You left *her* all alone?" Nico asked, sidling up to the woman. She smiled up at Nico, looking at him through her lashes. She nodded, faking sadness.

"I'll keep you company," Nico said, drunkenly leading her to the bar. She giggled and put her arms around him.

"Forget him." Kenny, the team's shortstop, said, waving them away. "Should we play another round?"

Jonas glanced at his watch. It was just after 11 PM. He didn't want to ruin the fun, especially since this was the most comfortable the team had been around him. But they had a game tomorrow and he had to be responsible. He was their boss. "I think it's time we wind down. Big game tomorrow."

Kenny threw his head back and groaned before saying, "Yes, sir. I'll go tell Romeo it's almost time to pack it in." He nodded toward the bar where Nico and the redhead were already making out. Jonas and the guys stood around the table talking about the next morning's game and finishing the last of their beers when they heard a commotion at the bar.

"Who is this?" a man shouted.

Jonas could hear Nico. "Sorry, man. We just met tonight."

"Ah, shit," Kenny said. "Sounds like our boy is in trouble."

Jonas began pushing his way through the crowd. The last thing he needed was one of his players getting hurt before a big game. Also, the last thing he needed was another incident with Nico. The guy was always getting into trouble.

As Jonas got closer to the bar, he could see a stocky man with a thick mustache glowering at Nico, as the redhead stood in the middle like a deer in headlights.

"Who the fuck are you?" the man asked Nico, shoving a finger into his chest.

Jonas was almost there. He just had to squeeze through a few more people.

"Ahh, you know what? I do know you. You're that hotshot pitcher," the man said sarcastically.

"You said it, man. Not me."

"Roger. Calm down," the redhead pleaded.

"You think you can just walk around Boston doing whatever you want because you throw a ball?" Roger asked, his face inches away from Nico's.

Jonas finally pushed his way through the onlookers and stood next to Nico. Roger backed up slightly.

"Why don't we just calm down a little," Jonas said, holding his hands up. "What's the problem here?"

"This punk had his tongue down my fiancée's throat," Roger said, nodding towards Nico.

Nico gave Jonas an innocent smile and a shrug.

"I see," Jonas said, looking at the redhead who wouldn't make eye contact.

"And who are *you*?" Roger asked, looking at Jonas.

"He's the guy your fiancée was trying to go home with before she found me," Nico said with a smile. "You really should keep a tighter leash on her."

"Nico," Jonas warned, shaking his head. Why did he have to open his mouth?

Jonas then watched everything unfold as if in slow motion. Roger brought his fist back and slammed it into Nico's left eye, causing him to fall backward into the barstools. The redhead screamed and covered her eyes. Nico was clambering to his feet as Roger approached him, carrying a barstool over his head.

"Let's see how you throw with a broken arm."

Jonas stepped in front of Roger and punched him in the stomach, causing him to double over and drop the barstool. He tried to stand upright and charge, but Jonas punched him again, this time square across the face. Security grabbed both of them, holding each back.

"Throw this man and his so-called fiancée out of my bar!" the bartender said firmly. Security let go of Jonas and led the couple out the doors. The patrons cheered as Jonas helped Nico up from the floor.

"Thanks, boss," Nico said as the bartender handed him some ice.

"You just had to open your mouth, didn't you?" Jonas said, annoyed.

Nico held the ice to his eye. "It's not my fault his girl has a wandering eye. The guy should know."

Jonas shook his head. He didn't understand what his father saw in Nico. His father had loved the kid, almost like his own son. He had seen him as some sort of underdog that he needed to help rise to the top. Jonas had been somewhat jealous of their relationship, but he would never admit it.

It was no mystery to anyone that the two didn't share the same relationship as the previous owner. Jonas was hard on Nico because he couldn't afford a player getting into any serious trouble. Sure, maybe it was a little more than that. Maybe it was out of spite, but he'd label it as tough love to anyone who questioned it.

"Let's get you home," Jonas said firmly.

"I can get myself home," Nico said, protesting.

"I don't trust you to."

Nico rolled his eyes and said goodbye to the rest of the team, who stood back, eyeing the situation from a distance. They all patted him on the back and said goodbye to Jonas.

As Jonas led Nico out the bar doors, he texted his driver to come to the curb and him up. After a minute or so, the black town car pulled up. His driver stepped out and opened the back passenger door. Nico ducked inside and Jonas followed.

"Where to, Mr. Matthews?" his driver asked.

Nico leaned forward and said his address—Mae's address.

It hadn't hit Jonas until just now. He had never been to her house before and was suddenly curious to see it, even if it was just from the outside.

The city lights whizzed by the darkened windows as they rode in silence. After a while, Nico said quietly, "Thanks for saving my ass tonight. That guy was huge."

"Just looking out for the team."

"You know, I meant to tell you congratulations earlier. Your dad would be proud."

Jonas nodded. The last thing he wanted to talk about was his dad, especially with Nico. Changing the subject, he asked, "Did you enjoy yourself at the party?"

"Definitely. Wendy went all out. Although my sister was my date."

"Not a bad one to have."

"True. Mae is one of a kind."

Jonas silently agreed. Nico didn't know about their history. If he did, he probably wouldn't be talking to him right now. Soon they pulled up to a white Victorian house with blue shutters. All the lights were off, except for a room upstairs. Jonas wondered what Mae was doing. Wondered if she was alone.

"Well, thanks for the ride," Nico said, opening the door and closing it behind him.

Jonas watched as Nico went inside. Jonas studied the house for a minute, and almost as if he willed her to appear, the front door opened. He watched as Mae walked barefoot toward the car, on her tiptoes. Her hair was damp and hung in waves, and she wore an oversized jersey. How did she always look so good?

"Mae," he said, almost as a question.

"Jonas." She stood, rubbing her arms to keep warm.

He opened the car door. "It's warmer in here."

Reluctantly, she slid inside and shut the door. Her bare legs grazed against him before she pulled them away. Being alone with her, and this close, he felt nervous. Tense. Expectant. He wondered if she felt it, too. He waited for her to say something.

"I just wanted to say thank you," she said, not meeting his gaze. "I know you two don't always see eye to eye."

"I did it for the team," Jonas said with a casual shrug.

She looked at him and furrowed her brow. "Why do you do that?"

"What?" he asked.

"Act like it's always about work. Like you can't just do something good."

Jonas didn't say anything. She sighed and opened the car door, sliding out.

Feeling bad, he called after her, "Mae."

"I'll see you tomorrow," she said, shutting the door and not looking back.

Jonas leaned his head back and let out a sigh. As he breathed in, the smell of her perfume lingered.

Chapter 4

Mae

Mae eased into her seat as the first pitch was thrown. The stadium erupted into chants and claps. There was an excitement in the air. It almost felt like a new hope just reverberating off the fans. Usually, she felt it, but today, her heart wasn't in it, which was surprising because Nico was in the starting lineup. Last night's moment with Jonas had kept her up most of the night and had trickled into today. Was it even a moment? All they did was make eye contact for a millisecond. She felt stupid for letting it get her all worked up and taking away from today.

Most days, she loved the sport. If her parents could see her now, they would be so happy to see her sitting in the owner's box. And if her parents could see Nico on the field, they would have been blown away. They had both worked in the industry and for this team. Her mother was a physical therapist for the team, and her father was an announcer. His dad jokes and warm personality made him a local celebrity.

Because of their parents' jobs, Mae and Nico were always at the games. She still remembered sitting behind the dugout, munching on popcorn, and screaming at the top of her lungs when the crack of a home run rang through the air. Some of her happiest memories were at this stadium. It was where she fell in love with baseball, and where she saw Nico realize what he wanted to do with his life. Baseball was in their blood.

She looked up at the sky and closed her eyes, hoping to feel her parents in some way. Sometimes, at the stadium, she would feel pangs of sadness hit her hard. After she lost them, she didn't go to the stadium for years. It was too difficult. There were too many memories. There were times she wanted to give up on baseball altogether, but Nico was set on becoming a pro. He was doing it for them, and how could she make him give it up? Now, she was fully immersed in the sport. She lived it, watched it, worked in it.

Mae opened her eyes and looked out over the field. This stadium held other memories too. This was where she met Jonas for the first time. She remembered meeting him in the dugout before her brother's first game. Beneath a baseball cap, his green eyes struck her first, followed by a soft smile surrounded by dark stubble. He was kind, a stark contrast standing next to his father, who was barking at the players. They didn't stay long, but an impression was made. He looked over his shoulder and gave her a look that said *I'm sorry* as he followed his dad out of the dugout.

"Earth to Mae," Nico said as he adjusted his laces.

"Sorry." She shook her head and resumed taking him through a few stretches she remembered her mom doing.

"That owner is a real piece of work," Nico said, nodding toward the entrance to the dugout. Despite their initial meeting, Nico grew to love Mr. Matthews. The tough love eventually turned into mutual respect. And the spark she felt for Jonas eventually turned into a wildfire that was put out as quickly as it began.

Out of the corner of her eye, she saw Jonas enter the owner's box. She took in a breath and held it for a second. She should be used to this by now. They saw each other practically every day at the office and every game day right here in this room. He looked good in a pair of black jeans and a white t-shirt. He wore a faded team cap and his five o'clock shadow was grown out a few days. It looked good on him.

Mae looked back out toward the field and pretended to be very intent on the game. She listened as his voice got closer, greeting everyone in the room. Her body tensed as her boss, Braydon, stood up and shook Jonas's hand. She could feel him, causing goosebumps to rise on her arms.

"Jonas. It's good to see you. That was a hell of a party last night," Braydon said.

"It sure was. I'm glad you enjoyed yourself," Jonas said.

"Maybe a little too much."

"Mae. Nice to see you."

She looked up and gave him a smile and a nod. "Jonas."

Jonas shoved his hands in his pocket and scooched down the row to an empty seat. A few minutes later, a perky blonde entered the box. She was introduced as the daughter of one of the bigwigs. Jonas offered her the seat next to him. *Of course, he did*, Mae thought. As much as she didn't want to be, Mae was tuned into their conversation

"Have you been in the owner's box before?" Jonas said.

"It's my first time."

"We have a virgin over here," Jonas said, raising a glass of beer.

The girl giggled. Mae rolled her eyes and adjusted in her seat. It was torture enough sitting in the same room. Hearing him badly flirt made it even worse.

"I'm hardly a virgin," the girl said coyly.

"You don't say," Jonas said, faking shock.

Mae let out a quiet sigh of disgust. Braydon turned and looked at her suspiciously.

"Did you see the call the ump made?" Mae lied, gesturing toward the field.

This seemed to satisfy her boss, who nodded and looked down toward the batter.

Mae listened to them talk a little more before she felt like her head was going to explode. She didn't know if it was the bad flirting or the creeping jealousy.

"Excuse me for a second. I have to use the ladies' room," Mae said, standing from her seat. Her only way out of the front row was sliding past the lovebirds. She felt her heart quicken as she passed her boss and approached Jonas. She usually avoided this close of contact, but this was unavoidable. She held her breath. As she brushed past him, she felt the small hairs on her neck stand up. Mumbling, "Excuse me," she quickly made it to the aisle and up the stairs to the box's exit. Out in the stadium, her heart rate slowed and she could breathe easier.

Mae walked toward the private restrooms and was relieved to find them empty. She leaned against the counter and studied herself in the mirror, shaking her head at her reflection. She was embarrassed about the hold he had on her, and the jealousy she had for someone who was barely legal. Was he trying to make her jealous? This unspoken thing with Jonas was getting ridiculous. Was it even a thing or was it all in her head?

Just then, the door to the bathroom swung open and the blonde girl entered. She saw Mae and walked over.

"Hi. I'm Amanda. Amanda Clark. I didn't get a chance to introduce myself earlier."

"Mae Klein," she said, mustering up a smile. "Nice to meet you."

"Mr. Matthews—er—Jonas said your brother is on the team?"

"Yeah, Nico. Number 21."

"How cool!"

Mae nodded.

"How lucky are you to do this every weekend. It's my first game, but I'm already in love. Those pants!" Amanda said, raising her eyebrows.

Mae couldn't help but laugh a little.

"Well, I'll see you in there," Amanda said before heading into an open stall.

"See ya!" Mae turned back to the mirror and adjusted her ponytail underneath her rose-pink cap. She tucked her wavy strands behind her ear and applied some clear gloss. Then she gave herself a little smile and internal pep talk before walking out.

Back in the owner's box, she saw Braydon and Jonas chatting by the bar.

"Mae! Come on over!" Braydon called out.

She smiled and hesitantly walked over to the pair. She was Braydon's personal assistant, but sometimes she felt like his life support. He was older and technically challenged, but besides that, he leaned on her for everything. Business and personal. He was in a messy divorce with his wife and currently fighting for custody of their twin girls. The wife wanted them with her in California, and Braydon wanted them in Boston because they'd grown up here. It definitely kept her busy, and in the office, she could use the distraction.

"What's up, boss?" she asked, pulling out her phone to be ready.

"Have a drink with us!" Braydon said loudly.

Mae could tell he was a little drunk.

"Can I get you a beer?" Jonas asked with a gentle shrug.

"Um, sure."

He ordered her favorite amber and tipped the bartender generously. Mae was impressed that he remembered. She felt a tiny flutter in her stomach. He handed her the icy glass.

"Thank you," she said, taking a sip. "Well, I'm going to go sit down."

"No, no. Stay. We were just discussing the upcoming event schedule," Braydon said.

"There's a lot going on," she said. And there was. There was the festival next week, the charity parties, the charity game, and the auction. It took a lot of convincing on her part to have the players offer themselves up as dates to bid on. In the end, they agreed, especially because the proceeds went to the children's leagues.

"I got everyone on board for the auction. I finalized the players yesterday," Mae said.

"Good girl. Thank you!" Braydon said, patting her on the back.

"That's going to be a real moneymaker," Jonas said.

"What about you, Jonas? Do you want to be auctioned off?" Braydon asked with a chuckle. "You could probably bring in some big bucks."

Jonas smiled and shook his head. God, she loved that smile. Shy and somehow confident at the same time.

"Are you seeing anyone?" Braydon asked, and at that moment, Mae really loved her boss. She was pretty confident the answer was *no*, but her curiosity was piqued anyway.

Jonas shook his head. "There's no time."

"Bullshit," Braydon said, finishing his beer and ordering another one. "I've been in this business a long time, Jonas. There's time if you make time. Plus, we're in *this* business. Women come easy."

"Braydon!" Mae said, giving him a little shove.

Her boss shrugged sheepishly. She rolled her eyes. He could be so thick-headed sometimes.

"That Amanda girl was cute," Braydon said suggestively.

"A little young, don't you think?" Mae said under her breath. Apparently, it wasn't quiet enough because Jonas sent her a look and her cheeks turned hot. Why had she said that? She hoped it didn't come off as sounding bitter.

Braydon's laughter cut through the awkwardness. "Mae! You little firecracker!" He held up his glass and clinked it against hers. She let out a hesitant laugh and took a sip of her beer.

"But really, Jonas. You don't want to be alone forever. You should really get out there," Braydon said, turning his attention back to Jonas.

"I'll think about it." Jonas looked down into his glass.

Mae could tell Jonas was uncomfortable with this conversation. Seeing him squirm was entertaining.

"What about you, Mae?" Braydon asked her, wiggling his eyebrows.

She nearly choked on her drink. It was fun watching Jonas squirm, but she didn't want to be in the same position. She saw Jonas stand up a little taller and look out at the field, squinting his eyes as if he was really focusing. He was definitely tuned in to *their* conversation, but was pretending not to be. She let out a little laugh. This could be fun.

"There are a couple prospects," she lied. "But no one's been able to lock me down yet." She winked at Braydon, and this answer seemed to satisfy her boss. Jonas cleared his throat and said, "I'm going to go sit down and watch the rest of the game."

Did she sense a hint of jealousy?

Chapter 5

Jonas

Was Mae really seeing someone? Or multiple people? These questions weighed on Jonas, even though they shouldn't. Especially since he was purposefully flirting with the blonde girl, Alyssa. Or was it Amanda? He couldn't remember, and he really didn't care that much. He had wanted to get under Mae's skin, but he wasn't expecting her to get right back under his. Whatever game they were playing was really getting to him.

The crowd in the stadium erupted into cheers, breaking him out of his thoughts. Nico had hit a winning home run in the tenth inning. Jonas stood with everyone else, cheering and clapping. Mae was beaming with pride. Her smile spread ear-to-ear and her brown eyes were filled with admiration as she looked down at her brother, who was running the bases. Jonas couldn't help but smile as he looked back at the field. She really was beautiful. Nico was lucky to have her as a sister. Anyone would be lucky to have her as something else.

Braydon patted him on the back. "Another win, Jonas! This is really shaping up to be your year."

"It's all them," Jonas said, gesturing toward the field.

"And partly me. For drafting them," Braydon said with a wink.

Once everyone finished celebrating and the stadium began clearing out, the group headed down to the dugout to congratulate the team. Mae hopped down with ease, and Nico scooped her up in a big hug. She really was part of the family. Jonas shook the players' hands and congratulated them on their win.

When he got to Nico, he held out his hand and shook firmly. "Nico. That was one hell of a hit."

"Thanks, boss. I credit a good night's rest. I left the bar shortly after you did last night."

"Glad to hear it." He saw Mae look between them both, raising an eyebrow. He couldn't blame her. His and Nico's relationship was often rocky. He knew he was tough on the kid, but he had to be. His father had been way too lenient. If Nico was going to live up to his full potential, he needed some tough love.

Jonas checked his watch and decided it was a good time to head back to the office to make his call to Nate. "I better head out."

"Stay, boss! Celebrate with us!" Nico said enthusiastically.

"Next time." Jonas said his goodbyes and walked up the stairs of the dugout toward the field exit. He heard the team pop a bottle of champagne and cheer. He smiled because they were one of the closest things he had to brothers.

Back at the empty office, he was allowed to gather his thoughts and the main points he wanted to bring up in this important phone call. Nate had given him his personal number at the party last night, but it was a Saturday, so he wasn't sure if he would even pick up. After a few rings, Nate's voice came on the line.

"Jonas. Do you ever take time off?"

Jonas laughed. "Not when there is something I really want."

"You are persistent. I'll give you that."

"Have I scared you off?"

"Not yet. What can I do for you?"

"Athletic wear. I want in." Jonas then went into business mode and listed off a few major points before Nate interrupted him.

"Okay, okay. You've convinced me."

"I have?" Jonas asked, surprised.

"I'm not saying we have a deal just yet, but you've got yourself a meeting. Call my secretary on Monday and set something up."

"Thank you, Nate. You won't regret this."

"Oh, and Jonas? Go enjoy the weekend."

"On it." Jonas hung up and let out a loud whoop. He'd finally done it. He'd secured a meeting. Jonas walked out of his office and strolled the empty hallways, soaking it all in. His celebration was last night, but he didn't truly feel like he had accomplished anything until now. Now he could celebrate. He wished he had someone to call to share the news. Someone who would know how much this moment meant. Mae flashed through his mind, but he couldn't call her. She probably wouldn't even pick up. He would have to celebrate on his own, and he knew just how to do it.

Jonas took the elevator down to the lobby and exited the high-rise, where Albert was waiting with the car. Jonas opened the back passenger door and slid inside.

"Where to, Mr. Matthews?" Albert asked, looking in the rearview mirror.

"Delaney's, please."

Albert nodded and put the car into drive. He eased away from the curb and drove the few miles to Jonas's favorite restaurant. Jonas stepped out of the car and walked toward the pillared building nestled in a large garden area. He loved this place because it didn't look like it belonged in Boston. He also loved the oysters paired with champagne. After pulling open the large glass door, he was immediately greeted by the hostess.

"Mr. Matthews. We weren't expecting you," she said, a little frazzled as she scrambled through her reservation book.

"No worries. This is an impromptu visit. Is there a table available?"

"Of course. Will there be anyone joining you this evening?"

"Just me."

"Right this way." The hostess grabbed a menu and led him toward the back of the restaurant.

"Is this booth okay?" she asked.

"This is perfect. Thank you." He slid into the booth and took the menu from her. He looked through it even though he already knew what he wanted.

"Mr. Matthews. It's great to see you," his waiter said as he sidled up to the table. "That was a great win today!"

"Thank you. It's looking to be a good season."

"Well, what can I get you this evening?" the waiter asked as he filled up Jonas's water glass.

"Can you please bring me a bottle of your finest champagne and the oysters, please?"

"Celebrating tonight?"

Jonas nodded.

"That will be right out. Should I put in an order for your usual ribeye with the bleu cheese wedge salad once you're finished with your first course?"

"You'd think I came here often," Jonas said with a laugh. "That would be great. Thank you."

Within a few minutes, a bottle of champagne on ice and a tray of oysters were delivered to the table. The waiter popped the champagne and poured a generous glass, then placed it on the table. Jonas thanked him and took his glass, leaning back against the comfortable leather of the booth. He took a sip and closed his eyes, satisfied. This was just what he needed.

Laughter came from a nearby booth. Jonas looked over and saw a couple sipping wine and sitting draped around each other. They looked happy. He had always wanted to bring someone special here to his favorite spot. He hadn't found anyone he wanted to share it with, besides Mae.

But since their relationship was only known to them, they'd stayed in the confines of their apartments.

Jonas's thoughts drifted to his conversation with Braydon in the owner's box earlier. *That was embarrassing*, he thought. Especially in front of Mae. Braydon could be so old-fashioned sometimes. He didn't understand that people weren't settling down young. They were focusing on their careers. It was the new way. Yet, he didn't know why he felt the need to prove himself to Braydon. Maybe it was because of his older age. He kind of felt like a father in his annoying way.

Braydon's old-fashioned views sometimes irritated Jonas, but he couldn't blame the guy. He was old himself and had been at the company far longer than Jonas. His father had hired Braydon and would rise from the grave if Jonas fired him. Plus, if Jonas were to let Braydon go, then Mae would probably go with him. She had been his personal assistant from the beginning. Where he went, she went. Despite his backward views, Braydon did know baseball. People called him a magician when it came to drafting players. He somehow always chose the best.

Still, Jonas couldn't shake the old man's words. He didn't know if the words bothered him or if it was because they were said in front of Mae. Maybe a little bit of both. Sure, Jonas would love to be celebrating with someone right now or go home to someone waiting for him. He just didn't know how to put business second.

Jonas tried to push his lonely thoughts away. Today was a good day. He took another sip of champagne and enjoyed his meal.

Back home, Jonas went to bed early, hoping it would clear his head. But come Monday, his thoughts were still eating away at him.

On his lunch break, he headed to the office gym to decompress. In the locker room, he changed out of his suit and into shorts and a muscle tank. Jonas laced up his running shoes and headed to the cardio area before stepping onto the treadmill and starting at a slow pace to warm up. Soon he was doing sprints, with beads of sweat dripping down his face. He was already feeling better. He slowed the pace and began sorting through his thoughts.

Jonas thought about his father's reputation in the office. It was no secret everyone hated him. His father was known to be power-hungry, bossy, and obsessed with work. Jonas thought about his father in their home life. Well, there wasn't much of a home life because his father was always at the office. Jonas was mostly raised by his mother and a nanny. When he spent time with his father, it was at the stadium. While Jonas was younger, he loved going to games because they had that time together. Once he was older, he couldn't stand being around him.

Jonas didn't want to be that man. He didn't want people to think he was Mr. Matthews 2.0. He would never want to be the most hated man in the office. Maybe if he was in a relationship, a serious relationship, people would look at him differently. He wouldn't be the power-hungry, work-obsessed boss. Perhaps he would seem a little more normal. Then Braydon would get off his back. His mom would, too.

But how? He didn't have time to date around and find *the one*. If that idea even existed. He didn't want to bother with dating apps or being set up by coworkers. Sure, there were women who were interested, like Braydon said. But they weren't in it for the right reasons. He at least wanted someone who was somewhat genuine. Or at least knew about baseball and the business he was in.

Jonas spotted Mae across the gym with Nico, talking to one of his trainers. She was deep in conversation, gesturing to Nico and replaying game highlights on her phone. Jonas was always impressed with her knowledge of the game and her commitment to Nico's career. Sure, maybe she was a little overprotective, but at least she genuinely cared.

Then it hit him. Mae. She would be perfect to start up a pretend relationship. They already knew each other, so it wouldn't come off too surprising to the rest of the office. They could say they were keeping their relationship private until they were ready to come out. It was the perfect plan.

Mae was the solution, but also the problem. There would be no way she would agree to this arrangement. Not with their history. He had broken things off with her because of their positions at work, but now his father was out of the way. Jonas was free to do what he wanted. He wasn't ready to settle down, but he sure could pretend he was. All he had to do was talk to Mae and convince her of his plan. It wasn't going to be easy, but he was sure he could sway her.

Chapter 6

Mae

Mae took a sip of lemon water as she waited for Braydon to show up for their lunch meeting. She checked the time on her phone and sighed. He was fifteen minutes late. She didn't know why she always showed up early, or even on time for that matter. Her boss was chronically late. It was a trait that was both annoying and endearing at the same time. He always had some excuse that he must have used his imagination to think up. Her favorite was when he said he ran into a famous older actress who wouldn't let him go until he gave her his number. Mae smiled to herself at the thought.

The waiter approached the table. "Still waiting on one more, miss?"

"Yes, I'm sorry. He should be here any minute."

"It's not a problem. Is there anything I can get you while you wait?"

"You know what? I can just put our order in. I know his favorites."

The waiter nodded and pulled out his pen and pad of paper.

"I will have the salmon salad with the lemon dressing. He will have the stuffed spinach and feta chicken."

"Sounds great. I'll have that out soon."

"Thank you," said Mae, handing him the menus.

As the waiter walked away, she saw Braydon enter through the revolving doors. He looked like his frazzled self when he was late. He approached the hostess stand. Mae held her hand up and gave a little wave. He spotted her and made his way over, took the seat across from her, and let out an exasperated sigh.

"You'll never believe what happened," he said theatrically.

"What was it this time? A zombie apocalypse?" asked Mae teasingly.

"Ha ha ha," he said sarcastically. "No really. Traffic jam on Pine Street. A man had fallen into the sewer. A worker must have left the manhole cover off."

"Oh, my gosh," exclaimed Mae, although she wasn't entirely sure if she believed him. She told herself she would check the news later.

"I know. I got here as fast as I could."

"No worries. I ordered our food just a moment ago. I got your favorite stuffed chicken."

"You know me too well. Thank you, Mae. Now, let's talk about the new players on the scene," Braydon said, pulling papers from his briefcase.

They went over stats and scores and college academics. Mae was always so impressed with Braydon's eye for good players. He saw things she didn't. She narrowed it down to intuition, as did everyone else. Braydon was known for his draft picks.

Their waiter brought the food and set it down carefully around the paperwork. They worked through lunch, taking bites and creating the ideal drafts for the team. Once confident in their choices, Braydon filed his paperwork back into his briefcase, and they finished the last bites of their meals.

"That was a productive and delicious meeting," said Braydon, patting his stomach.

Mae nodded, wiping her mouth gently with her napkin.

"And look who walked in," he said, nodding toward the entrance.

Mae turned and saw Jonas at the hostess stand with a tall man who looked very familiar, but she couldn't place him. She hoped Jonas wouldn't see them and would be seated at a table across the restaurant. She knew better, though, as Braydon shouted, "Jonas! Over here!"

Jonas looked up from talking to the hostess and gave a nod. Mae sank a little in her chair.

"Braydon, fancy seeing you here," said Jonas, somewhat sarcastically. This was Braydon's favorite restaurant.

"You have Delaney's. I have Ivy," said Braydon with a chuckle as he stood to shake hands. Mae reluctantly stood as well to greet them. Jonas held her hand a beat too long and looked at her more intensely than he had years. She squirmed in her cream dress and cleared her throat. Why was he looking at her like that? Had Braydon noticed? She quickly sat back in her seat and took a sip of water. She couldn't even pay attention to what the three men were talking about because she was drowning in the look Jonas had just given her.

After a minute, she heard her name being spoken.

"Mae?"

"Hmm?" She looked from Braydon to Jonas.

"Can you?" asked Jonas, raising an eyebrow.

"Can I what?" She had clearly missed part of the conversation.

"Can you stay and have a quick meeting with me?   It   won't   take   long."

"Uh, sure. Is that okay with you, Braydon?" she asked hesitantly, before turning to her boss. She was hoping he would say they had too much work to do at the office.

Instead, to her dismay, he said, "Sure, take all the time you need."

"Thank you, Braydon."

"We're actually all wrapped up here. I'm going to head back to the office," said Braydon, signaling for the check.

"I'll meet you at the bar," Jonas said to Mae before walking away with the man he came with. She watched them shake hands at the door. It bothered Mae that she couldn't figure out where she knew the man from. Maybe if she had been listening, and not lost in her own thoughts, she would have caught his name.

Braydon signed the check and stood, collecting his phone and briefcase. "Well, you better head over there. Don't want to keep our boss waiting," he said, nodding toward the bar.

Mae nodded. "Thank you for lunch. I'll see you back   at   the   office."

Braydon gave a little wave and headed toward the door. Mae sat for a moment longer, collecting herself. What could Jonas possibly need to meet with her for? They worked adjacent to each other, but never actually together. Whatever he needed was communicated through Braydon. The distance was better that way and they both knew it. She took another sip of water and glanced over at Jonas. His back was to her.

Opening her purse, she found her compact and took a quick glance at her appearance. She checked her teeth and put on a light coat of lipstick, then felt someone watching her. Mae looked up and saw Jonas smirking. Had he been watching her? Her cheeks burned. She tried to brush aside her embarrassment and stood casually. She smoothed her dress and grabbed her purse before making her way over to the bar.

"All right, Jonas. What do you need?" she asked with a sigh, taking a seat beside him.

"Whoa, whoa. Slow down. Let's have a drink first," said Braydon, holding his hands up.

"It's still a workday, you know."

"And I'm your boss."

Mae rolled her eyes. "Whatever you say, *boss.*"

Jonas signaled the bartender.

"What can I get you, Mr. Matthews?" he asked.

Does everyone in this city know who he is? Mae thought to herself. It was irritating and sexy at the same time.

"I will take a scotch and she will have a glass of sauvignon blanc."

The bartender nodded and went to get their drinks.

Mae wanted to be annoyed with him for ordering for her, but also found it endearing that he remembered her favorite wine.

As if reading her thoughts, Jonas asked, "Wine's okay, right?"

She nodded.

"We'll have to save the jalapeno margaritas for another time," he said with a wink.

She shook her head at him, trying to hold in a smile. Mae remembered the weekend trip they took to Mexico. It was during the off season and had been a spontaneous decision. It was really the only time they were out in public as a couple. In another country, they had felt far enough away from their coworkers and Jonas's father.

They stayed at a beautiful, beachside, five-star resort and had barely left the room. The one night they did come up for air, they dined at the resort's restaurant with a candlelit dinner. Afterward, they went up to the rooftop bar and ordered one too many jalapeno margaritas. Mae had never laughed so hard. They stumbled along the beach, stealing kisses, and wound up going for a night swim fully clothed. She had felt so free, and so happy.

Looking at Jonas now, it was hard to believe they were ever those two people.

"What happened in Mexico, stayed in Mexico," she said, shooting him a playful look. But she felt a tinge of sadness as she said it. His eyes seemed to briefly reflect that same sadness before he blinked and looked at the bartender, who was approaching with their drinks.

"Our finest scotch and a brand-new sauvignon blanc. You're the first to try it, miss," said the bartender, setting their drinks down on the marble bar top.

"Wow. Thank you," said Mae appreciatively.

Jonas gave the man a nod and turned to face her. He held his drink up.

"Cheers, Mae," he said with a twinkle in his eye. He was up to something, but Mae held her glass out and clinked it to his.

"So, now that we have our drinks. What's this about?"

Jonas took a sip of his scotch.

Suddenly, a thought occurred to her. "Is it Nico?" she asked worriedly.

Jonas held up his hand and shook his head as he swallowed his drink. "No, no."

She waited for him to continue.

"I have a proposition for you," said Jonas, looking down into his glass.

"A proposition?" she asked, confused. "But I'm happy in the position I am. I could never leave Braydon."

"Not that kind of proposition."

"What are you talking about, Jonas?" she asked. Curiosity was starting to make her impatient.

"I want you to marry me," he said, meeting her eyes.

She nearly dropped her glass of wine.

"You what?"

"Hear me out. It wouldn't be a *real* marriage. It would just be for show."

"What the hell are you talking about, Jonas?" she said, her voice rising.

"We'll say we eloped. We'll say we've been seeing each other secretly for a while now, and—"

"Jonas! Stop!" she said, nearly shouting. He was rambling on nonsensically. Mae felt like she was in a strange dream.

He stopped talking for a moment and she felt like she could breathe again. She waited for an explanation as he took a deep breath.

"The office will never respect me fully if they think I'm a clone of my father. I need to look like I have it all together. I need my life to look balanced—work and 'love,'" he said, making quotation marks with his fingers as he said 'love.'

Mae couldn't believe what she was hearing. This had to be a joke.

"Then go on a date. Find a wife the real way," she said.

"I don't have time for that," he said, shaking his head. "Plus, you're easy."

Mae slapped him across the face. She couldn't believe she had done it. It felt like a reflex. She felt the eyes of the patrons of the restaurant on them, but she didn't care. She was seeing red. Grabbing her purse, she stood from her barstool. Jonas's hand slipped around her wrist as she turned to leave. She looked back at him, tears in her eyes.

"Mae, I didn't mean it like that," he said quietly, his eyes full of apologies. "I just meant I know you. We have history."

"Well, I'm not going to be a part of *that* future," she said, pulling her arm out of his grasp. She began to walk away.

"You'll give in, Mae. I have Nico, don't I? And I can easily get him moved back down to the minors, or to Florida, or somewhere else horrible," he said after her. She couldn't believe he was threatening her. *What did I ever see in him?* she wondered as she left the restaurant.

Chapter 7

Jonas

After Mae abruptly walked out on Jonas, he had sat at the bar in slight disbelief. He couldn't believe he had actually done it. He had proposed his secret plan to her. But he also couldn't believe she had slapped him. Or could he? Jonas coolly sat there going over the event, trying to ignore the eyes of everyone around him. Could he blame them? They just witnessed a soap opera scene play out before them. He rubbed his cheek where her hand had struck him. It still slightly stung. He downed the rest of his scotch.

"Would you like another, Mr. Matthews?" the bartender asked hesitantly, looking toward the exit where Mae had just left.

Jonas shook his head. "That's all right. I'll take the check."

The bartender nodded and started typing on the register, sneaking glances at Jonas. "She was a fiery one," he said with a small smirk.

"You have no idea," Jonas said with a sigh.

"What did you do to piss her off?"

"I proposed to her," Jonas said with a laugh.

The bartender's eyes widened as he laid the check on the counter.

"So, I'm assuming there won't be any wedding bells in the near future."

"We'll see about that," Jonas said with a wink. He stood from his barstool and shrugged his jacket over his broad shoulders. Scribbling on the tab, he left a generous tip on top of what he owed. As he headed for the exit, most everyone avoided eye contact. Jonas walked through the revolving door and found his town car waiting.

"Mr. Matthews," his driver said as he started to get out of the driver's seat.

"No need today, Albert," said Jonas, holding up his hand.

"But—"

"I'm going to walk." He tossed a wad of cash and Albert caught it. "Go grab some lunch. Swing by the office around six. I should have everything wrapped up by then."

"Thank you, sir," Albert said, nodding graciously.

Jonas needed the walk to clear his head, but he couldn't fight the memories that swarmed him. He remembered the weekend away with Mae. Clinking their glasses together as the mariachi played. Walking on the beach, holding her hand, as they were unsteady on their feet. Being pushed around by the waves, laughing hysterically. Gently helping her out of her soaking wet dress and into the California king-sized bed. It was one of the best weekends of his life. He was away from the pressure of work and the watchful eye of his father.

On the plane ride home, she had fallen asleep on his shoulder. Looking down at her, he had come to the decision that he would come clean with his father and the entire office. If she was open to it, of course. He was mostly confident she would be happy to be out in the open with everything, even though they never really talked about it. They were happy in their little bubble. She never pressured him to come out of it.

When he went back to the office on Monday, his father had called him into his office. "Did you have a nice weekend?" his father asked with a slight sneer.

"I did. Thank you."

"You take this job seriously, don't you, Jonas?"

"Yes, sir. Of course."

"I only ask because I'm not really seeing that from you."

"Because I took a weekend off?" Jonas said, raising an eyebrow.

"You think I got to where I am by taking weekends off?" his father asked, gesturing to his office.

Jonas shook his head. He knew his father never took weekends off, let alone time off. He was either in the office or at the ballpark. He had prioritized long work hours, and it had cost him his wife and his family. Yet, he stood here proudly. Smugly.

"No, sir," Jonas said, shaking his head. Even though he was a grown man, his father still treated him like a child.

"So, what was *sooo* important?"

"I just needed some time away."

His father let out a laugh. "More like, needed to get laid in Mexico."

Jonas gulped. Did his father know about Mae?

His father continued. "Whoever you took, I hope she was worth it and that you got it out of your system."

Jonas breathed a small sigh of relief. He didn't know it was Mae.

"Yes, sir."

"Men like us can't be tied down to anything besides success. Remember that, Jonas."

Jonas nodded solemnly.

"You can see yourself out," his father said, getting back to the papers on his desk.

As much as he had hated his father, Jonas was now slowly, but surely, becoming him. He hoped the success was worth it. It had to be.

When he made it back to his office, he gulped a glass of water and slammed it down on his desk. Even though he had walked several blocks, he was still coming down from that explosive encounter with Mae. He didn't know he was going to run into her at the restaurant and hadn't had time to completely plan what he was going to say in terms of his proposed arrangement, but he didn't want to lose this opportunity. Sure, his delivery could have been better, but either way, it was a bomb he had dropped on her.

He had thought if he brought up some better memories of their past it may soften her up a bit, but he had seen the hurt that flashed through her eyes. She wasn't completely over it. Maybe reminders of what once was were not a wise choice. He had felt that hurt for a brief moment, too, but he tried his best to hide it. Hopefully she didn't see.

Jonas closed his eyes and leaned back in his chair, letting more memories wash over him.

What they'd had was good, but he could not be distracted by it. Was she the right choice for this scheme? Was there *too* much history? He let out a sigh and sat up straight. It had been good, but it was over. He had to leave the past in the past, and see this as strictly business.

He wasn't an idiot. Yes, this was asking the impossible of her, but Jonas also knew he had the leverage he needed to make it possible. Nico. Was it fair to do that to her? No, but he knew how to get what he wanted—right or wrong.

After his lunch with Nate, he now had leverage there, too. Nate had had a few too many scotch and sodas at their business meeting, which Jonas had purposefully planned at a rooftop bar. He knew liquor would loosen things up a little bit. Little did he know it would loosen Nate's lips.

After discussing his proposal, it didn't seem like Nate was completely sold yet. With a frown, he remembered the conversation.

"You know, I had actually wanted to work with your father years ago."

"Really?" Jonas asked curiously. He had no idea.

"Yeah, but he shut that idea down real quick. He was a piece of work, your dad."

Jonas sighed. "You have no idea."

"Family is complicated," Nate said, taking a long sip of his drink.

Jonas waited for him to continue.

"I have a younger brother, you know? Just found out."

"Really?" Jonas asked, intrigued.

"Yep. All of Boston knew my father was a cheater. Everyone but my mother at the time."

Jonas pretended to be surprised, but he knew Nate's father's reputation.

"Apparently, he wasn't careful enough. He planted his seed with some woman on the Back Bay," Nate said, finishing his drink and signaling the bartender for another.

"How did you just now find out?" Jonas asked.

"My dad was very good at keeping secrets and paying money to keep them buried. My mother finally pulled her head out of the sand and hired a private investigator years ago. I just now found the files."

The bartender brought over Nate's drink, as he continued. "He's actually on your team."

"Who?" asked Jonas, confused.

"My brother," Nate said, slurring a little. "Kenny Michaels."

"*Kenny* is your brother?" asked Jonas, almost choking on his drink.

"Yep. He's been in this city the whole time. Right in front of me."

"Does *he* know?"

"No. I haven't decided what to do with this information. My mother would be destroyed if she knew I knew."

But Jonas knew what he could do with this information. It would be leverage. This could be just what he needed to solidify a deal. He felt a small tinge of guilt, but he pushed it aside. He had to do whatever it took.

After drinks, Jonas thought it best he took Nate downstairs to the restaurant to sober up. He wasn't completely heartless. After seeing Nate was in no condition to sit down for an actual meal, Jonas placed an order to go with the hostess. That was when he saw Braydon and Mae, and everything seemed to fall into place for him.

Shaking himself from his memory of the day, Jonas started going through the paperwork on his desk. He had a report he needed to submit to the league by four that afternoon. He spent the next hour going through the team's stats and putting together his report. Once he was finished, he was about to hit *send* when the door burst open. Mae walked through the doorway seething, with Wendy running after her.

"I'm so sorry, Mr. Matthews. She just stormed right by me and—" Wendy said frantically.

"It's okay, Wendy," he said, nodding. "I'll handle it."

Wendy nodded hesitantly.

"Okay," she said, looking between them confusedly. "Well, let me know if you need anything." She backed out of the office, closing the door behind her.

He sat back in his chair and clasped his hands together, studying Mae. She didn't say anything. He knew she was angry. Jonas knew that silent temper of hers. She began pacing his office and he watched her, amused. He knew he was about to get what he wanted and was enjoying every second of it. He was also enjoying watching her curves in that cream dress as she walked back and forth. He had always loved that dress.

"What can I do for you, Mae?" he asked with a side smile.

She shot him a look. "Don't smile at me, Jonas. Unless you want another red cheek."

He pressed his lips together and tried to fight a smile, faking seriousness.

She stopped pacing for a moment and glared at him. "I'll do it on one condition."

"And what's that?" he asked.

"I want you to, in writing, promise that Nico can in no way be harmed by you if I agree to this. And I will want to have my lawyer look it over before I sign it."

Jonas nodded. "Is that all?" he asked.

"Yes. That seems entirely fair, after what you're asking me to do."

As much as he didn't care for Nico, his hate had subsided over the past year. Enough time had passed that Jonas had almost forgotten his father had almost left Nico the team. Jonas had only found out after reading the drafts of his father's will. He couldn't believe that his father had even thought about leaving *his* legacy to this brat. This hot shot. This boy who had no relation to his father.

Finding this out made Jonas somehow hate his father even more after death. In the end, his father had left him the company and the team. Still, Nico nagged his thoughts. What was so special about him? It was this resentment that made their relationship rocky, as much as Jonas tried to keep it professional. Still, a deal was a deal. He had to agree to Mae's conditions in order for this to work.

"Okay."

"Okay," she said sarcastically.

"Perfect. Now sit down, because I want you to know my conditions," he grinned.

Chapter 8

Mae

Mae pulled into her driveway and clicked the garage door opener. As it slowly opened, she leaned her head against the seat and let out a sigh. It was dark out and the stars were shining. Out here in the suburbs, you could see them. They didn't have to compete with city lights. She glanced at the dash. It was just after eight. The meeting with Jonas had taken much longer than she expected. He had laid out plenty of conditions for their arrangement, which was not only aggravating, but time-consuming.

Mae had left frustrated and overwhelmed. She was thankful to see Nico's truck wasn't in the garage. She needed some time alone to think. Easing the car into the garage, she put it in park, grabbed her purse from the front seat and opened the door to the house. It was quiet and dark. The solitude was just what she needed to work through her emotions that were at an all-time high right now.

She walked to the living room and turned on the lamp by the couch. Seeing a photo of herself and her mother, she picked it up and ran her thumb over her mom's face.

"Oh, Mom. I wish you were here," she said softly. "You would probably tell me I was crazy for even agreeing to this." Mae shook her head and set the photo back down on the table. She ran her fingers over the other framed photos sitting neatly on the table. She stopped when she came to Nico's. It was his first team photo from middle school. He looked so happy. Little did he know everything would change just a year later when the police would deliver the news.

Through the years, Mae had done her best to raise him. She had sacrificed so much to be the mother figure he needed. She also tried to keep things as normal as possible by staying in this house. Sure, it was dated. She and Nico had a hard time changing anything because it felt wrong. As much as it was a blast from the past, it had charm and warmth.

She walked through the living room, gently running her fingers across the walls. She was trying to soak it all in, as these could very well be her last moments here. She sat down at the bottom of the stairs and put her head in her hands. Hot, angry tears filled her eyes.

What was she doing? She was better than some pawn in someone else's scheme. She was better than letting the man she once loved use her this way. But she was also Nico's sister, and she'd been taking care of him for the last ten years. She wasn't about to let some conniving big shot take everything away from her little brother. Not if she could stop it.

Her phone rang. It was Nico. She tried to gather herself. She wiped her eyes, even though he couldn't see her.

"Hey, Nico. What's up?"

"Hey, sis. I just got out of practice and some of the guys wanted to grab a few beers."

"Okay? Are you asking my permission?"

Nico paused. "Uh, no. I don't know. I just thought I would let you know it might be a late night."

"Nico, you're a big boy. You can do what you want," she said matter-of-factly.

"I know that. Jeez. What's up with you?"

Mae sighed. "Nothing. Sorry. It was just a long day at work."

"Okay, well, get some rest."

"Have fun."

"Thanks," he said, hanging up.

"Be safe," she said softly, putting her phone down.

Maybe it was time to cut the cord. As much as she wanted to protect her brother from everything, he did need to grow up a little. Okay, a lot. Plus, this house was too big for the two of them. She held her fingers to her temples and pressed. Her head hurt. This was too much happening all at once. Damn you, Jonas, for expediting all these decisions she wasn't ready to make.

Mae walked to the wine rack and pulled out a nice red blend she had picked up at the corner market last week. She had yet to indulge in it, but tonight felt like the perfect night. She unscrewed the cork and poured a generous serving in a wine glass. It was good, but would be better enjoyed in pajamas in bed.

She made her way upstairs to her bathroom and turned on the shower. Soon, steam was creeping up the glass doors and she stepped inside, trying to wash off the day. Out of the shower, she rummaged through her dresser for a pajama set. She stepped into it and grabbed her wine, setting it on her nightstand. Sliding under the sheets, Mae put on a show to zone out to. This was just what she needed.

After she finished her glass of wine and an episode of a dating reality show, she brushed her teeth and turned out the lights. But when she closed her eyes, she saw Jonas, which frustrated her.

"Whyyyy?" she groaned. She tried her best to think of other things, but he kept intruding on her thoughts. And when she finally drifted to sleep, Jonas met her there, too. In his office.

It was late. Dusk had settled over the city, and the lights shone through the office windows. Jonas sat in the black leather chair at his desk, looking through the paperwork Mae had set on his desk. She waited rather impatiently for him to dismiss her so she could head home. Besides his secretary, Wendy, they were the only ones in the office.

Mae studied Jonas as he studied the papers. His brow furrowed as he ran his fingers through his dark hair. She loved when he did that. It was what he did when he was stressed or nervous. Despite his efforts, it would just fall back in place.

"Does everything look okay?" she asked, shuffling her feet.

"Yes. I'm just making sure these stats match up with the coach's."

Mae nodded. She was ready to go home. She glanced at her phone. It was after seven.

"Have somewhere to be?" Jonas asked, raising an eyebrow and nodding at her phone.

"No, sorry. It's just getting late. Don't you want to go home?" she asked.

"There's nothing to go home to," he said softly.

She felt bad for him for a brief second, until she remembered that this was the life he asked for. He chose success over a personal life. Over love. Over her.

He nodded toward the bar. "This could be a while. Why don't you pour yourself a drink?"

"I'm working."

"It's Friday. Go on. Pour me a whiskey while you're at it. The one on the top right shelf."

Mae rolled her eyes and walked to the bar. If she had to be here late, she might as well enjoy it a little. She poured his whiskey and settled on white wine for herself. She set his drink on his desk and took a seat across from him.

He slid the papers over so she could look at the numbers. She sipped on her wine as she compared the spreadsheets. She could feel Jonas looking at her, but didn't look up. For the next hour, they worked together circling discrepancies and making notes. She was two drinks in. Probably not wise when trying to be meticulous.

"I better catch up," Jonas said, eyeing her glass of wine. He stood and walked to the bar behind her. She heard him pour another glass. Soon, she felt him close. Too close. His breath was on her neck, and a shiver ran down her spine. He pointed at a figure on the spreadsheet. "Highlight this one."

She couldn't help but feel disappointed as she grabbed a highlighter and marked the page. Was she the only one who felt the tension in the air? It was like static. They hadn't been alone together like this in years.

"Anything else?" she asked, almost holding her breath. His face was still close to hers.

When he didn't say anything, she turned to look at him. Her eyes traveled down to his lips. Big mistake. His mouth was on hers within seconds. She let his lips massage against hers briefly before pushing him away gently. "Jonas," she said, searching his face. There was something in his eyes. Almost carnivorous. It was all she needed.

She pulled the collar of his shirt and brought his lips to hers. He parted her lips with his tongue desperately and explored her mouth. When they came up for air, she gently bit his bottom lip before pulling away and giving him a mischievous smile. He let out a groan.

Abruptly standing, Jonas walked swiftly to the office door and closed it. He turned the lock. Mae gulped.

"But Wendy…" she protested.

"Fuck Wendy," he said. He pulled her out of the armchair and pushed her gently against his desk. Jonas pressed his body against hers and she could feel his erection through his pants. He leaned down and kissed her behind her ear and crept down her neck. Her hands were in his hair, pulling desperately. She needed to be closer. Her hands moved down his chest and met his erection. She massaged him slowly.

"Fuck," he said, throwing his head back in pleasure.

Mae smiled with satisfaction. She loved having this power over him.

He looked back down at her intently. He placed his hands on her thighs and quickly shoved them under her skirt. When fingers met her lace panties, he slowed down. Slowly and rhythmically, he rubbed against her. She let out a soft moan and gasped when he dipped a finger inside her. He pressed his forehead to hers as they breathed roughly together. Their eyes locked as continued dipping his fingers in and out of her, until she felt like she was close to the edge. She couldn't let herself go yet. She needed more.

She reached for his belt and unbuckled it. Jonas lifted her onto the desk, so she was sitting with her legs wrapped around him. She undid the clasp of his pants, pulling them down until the tip of his erection was touching her just so. She shuddered. He pulled her panties to the side and entered her slowly, allowing just his tip to enter her. Mae let out a moan. He entered her again. More this time, but not filling her completely.

She couldn't take it. She leaned back, opening her legs more, and watched his eyes take her in. He grabbed her panties and pulled them off, tossing them aside. He then grabbed her thighs and slammed into her suddenly, taking her breath away. Then he was suddenly going slow. She grinded against him, following his rhythm. Mae felt herself peaking and gripped the edge of the desk as she threw her head back.

"Mae," he whispered, and she felt him tense inside her.

She pushed herself harder onto his erection.

"Mae," he said louder as he pulled out and plunged into her again. She felt him throbbing. Releasing. She let herself go, too.

Mae sat up in bed, breathless. It was just a dream. Nevertheless, she was wet. She groaned and grabbed a pillow, placing it over her head.

"Damn you, Jonas."

This marriage was a bad idea.

Chapter 9

Jonas

Jonas sat in his home office, sipping a cup of hot coffee. The steam crept up and fogged up his glasses. He took them off and wiped them with the sleeve of his robe before placing them back on the bridge of his nose. He checked the time. It was five on a Sunday morning, and a rare day off from the office. Despite this, he still had work to do.

He had been up all night typing up notes for the agreement he would enter with Mae. He had to work quickly and send it off to his lawyer in case Mae changed her mind. Of course, he was using his private lawyer. The team's lawyer was obviously out of the question. He typed a few more notes into the margins and sent it in an email to his lawyer.

As he heard the swish of the email being sent, he stood from his desk and made his way back to his bedroom. His California king-size bed sat plush on a large wooden canopy bedframe. The white, crisp Egyptian sheets were calling his name after the night he had. He took the last sip of his coffee and placed it on his nightstand before crawling under the sheets.

He lay back and put his hands behind his head, closing his eyes. As tired as he was, too many thoughts were trickling into his head. He wondered how the office would react when he and Mae made their announcement. The plan was to go public on the first night of the festival. Their news would really kick things off.

In his office that day, when she agreed to his scheme, he laid out his master plan. Or at least what he had come up with so far.

"So how are we doing to do this?" Mae had asked skeptically.

"We will say we eloped one weekend."

"Newsflash. You never take a day off. No one will believe that."

Jonas realized she was right. "True. Well, we will both take this weekend off, and no one will be the wiser."

"That's too short of notice. Braydon will flip," said Mae, crossing her arms. He could tell she was being difficult on purpose.

"Don't worry about Braydon. I'll lend him Wendy. Plus, I'm his boss, remember?"

"Yes, you've made it clear you're *everyone's* boss," she said, rolling her eyes. "So what? We are going to elope this weekend?"

"Yes, except we aren't *actually* going anywhere. We will be hiding out in our homes."

"You know Nico lives with me. That won't work."

"Then I'll put you up in a hotel for the weekend."

Jonas watched as Mae pursed her lips and thought for a moment

"The Ritz," she finally said.

"What?" Jonas asked, raising an eyebrow.

"I want to stay at the Ritz with your card on file," said Mae with a smirk.

She was definitely going to take advantage of this situation. He couldn't help but smirk. Maybe she was *almost* as bad as he was.

"Fine," he said.

She sat back in her chair and lifted her chin triumphantly.

"So where are we 'eloping?'" she asked, making air quotations with her fingers.

"Mexico," he said confidently.

"Of course you'd choose Mexico," she said under her breath.

"We both know it. We both have memories from there. It will make it more believable. We can even tell the story of swimming with our clothes on."

"No way," she said, shaking her head. "I'm not sharing those details, especially with my brother or my boss."

"Come on, Mae. We have to make it look *real*. Plus, people will think it's cute," he said with a shrug.

"Nothing about this is cute."

"If you're not going to sell it, then it will be Nico who suffers. You know the draft is coming up. I can easily drop him—"

"No," said Mae sharply. She looked up at him with defiance. "You're diabolical."

Jonas let her words pierce him before brushing it off. He simply shrugged.

"Tell your lawyer to email mine," said Mae, standing from her chair and walking out of his office. Clearly the conversation was over.

Nico was her weak spot and Jonas knew exactly how to use it to his advantage. He imagined the look on Nico's face when they made their announcement. Would it be shock? Disgust? Anger? Probably all three. Jonas couldn't help but smile. As much as Nico was Mae's weakness, she was just as much his. She was all he *really* had, and Jonas was about to take her away from him. Now Nico would know how it felt to come second, just like Jonas did with his father.

As if that wasn't satisfying enough, Braydon would be there, too. Jonas could gently rub it in his face that he, in fact, does have a life outside of work, and it's with his own personal assistant. The old man will think he's losing it. As for the rest of the office, he imagined they would be happy for them. This whirlwind romance would show there is a different side to Jonas. He would show he is different from his father. At least, for show. Maybe they would respect him more as a hard-working and doting husband.

There could be other benefits to this arrangement. Jonas hadn't been with a woman in a while. Well, not in a serious way. There had been one-night stands. Nothing special. He was a man with needs, after all. He didn't have to work very hard at it, being one of the most successful bachelors in Boston. One-night stands were easy. There were no *real* emotions. No ties. When the night was over, he was back to focusing on what was important. Work.

The truth was, he hadn't had anything serious since Mae. After ending things with her, he refused to let anyone get too close again. It was too complicated. Too messy. Plus, no one really compared to her. Even though he kept denying there was anything serious to begin with, they were now about to take the most serious step.

He wondered, but highly doubted, if any of their old chemistry would come back to the surface. Dirty thoughts popped into his mind, and he laughed to himself. There was no way Mae would let him get close to her in that way again. He would have to get his needs met on the side. There wasn't anything an NDA couldn't cover up. Mae would understand. She already thought he was awful. She wouldn't be surprised if he was unfaithful to their fake marriage. What was it she had called him? Diabolical. If she already thought it, why try to be anything different?

After working through all the thoughts in his head, Jonas finally fell asleep knowing his plan was going accordingly. He slept most of the day and night, peaceful and content. He could get used to these weekends off.

The next two days were busy in the office, preparing for the draft and the upcoming charity festival. He had been holed up in his office with meetings. He had barely seen Mae and she made no acknowledgement that she had received the agreement from his lawyer. Everything almost seemed normal. Like he hadn't asked her to marry him. Had she decided to back out? If she did, his whole plan would be foiled. She had to know it would not be a wise decision with the upcoming draft. He could replace Nico easily with an up and comer. Sure, he would receive a lot of backlash for it from everyone, including the city of Boston, but he was the owner. He had the final say.

That evening, he was working late, looking through the final picks Braydon had brought to him. Usually, Mae was the one who swiftly dropped papers off without a word, as that was her job as Braydon's personal assistant. She was avoiding him more than usual. Jonas was now convinced that Mae had backed out. He sighed and stood from his desk, walking toward the mirrored bar in the corner of his office. He pulled down a bottle of vodka and poured a generous glass, feeling his throat burn from the first sip.

What was his new plan? Would he follow through with making Nico's life hell? He never thought he would actually have to go through with it. Yet, Jonas was a man of his word and needed to be taken seriously, even if it hurt Mae. He placed his glass on the counter and pressed his fingers to his temples. He had to think.

Suddenly, he heard a light knock on the door. He thought everyone had gone home already.

"Wendy, I thought you had gone home," he said, still facing the bar.

He heard the door slowly swing open. "It's not Wendy."

Jonas spun around and saw Mae standing there. She had a smile on her face. He felt his stomach drop. Not only was she here in his office, but she was smiling? This was unexpected. What was going on? He felt like a bomb was about to be dropped.

"I wasn't expecting you," he said.

"We had an agreement, didn't we?" she asked, holding up papers.

The agreement. He nodded. Jonas tried to fight the satisfaction he was feeling because he wanted to come off cool and confident. He casually took a sip of his drink before pouring a splash more.

"Would you like a drink?" he asked, motioning to the liquor on the shelves. "I have wine chilling as well."

"No, thank you. I'm strictly here on business," she said, holding her hand up before taking a seat in front of his desk. She crossed her legs and smoothed out her dress. She looked good.

Jonas took a seat at his desk, across from her.

"I take it everything looked all right?" he asked, nodding toward the papers she had placed on his desk.

"Yes. My lawyer and I went through everything yesterday morning. You were very specific."

"You have to be in these agreements."

"Right. Because these agreements are the norm," she said sarcastically.

"I think you'd be surprised. Hollywood is full of marriages that are for show."

"Well, should we sign it?" Mae asked, trying to hide her hesitation.

"Ladies first," said Jonas, grabbing a pen from his desk and sliding it over to her.

She caught his eye for a moment before picking up the pen and turning to the last page. He heard her take a deep breath as she scribbled her signature on the line. She slid the papers to Jonas and handed him the pen. He added his signature and stacked the papers carefully before placing them in a manila envelope. It was done.

"I'll have my lawyer send you the signed copies. Make sure you put them somewhere safe. Somewhere hidden. I don't want anything coming out," said Jonas, as he locked the envelope away in his desk.

Mae nodded.

"So, are you ready for this?" asked Jonas, leaning back in his chair. He wasn't sure if he wanted to know the answer.

"Mhmm," she said with a smirk. "The question is—are *you* ready?"

"Me? Of course. I'm the one who proposed this agreement."

"Well, I hope you know what you're getting into. I just put our house on the market and Nico moved in with his best friend."

Jonas gulped. Obviously, they had to make their marriage look real, and living separately would raise suspicion. Still, he wondered if he had thought this all through. He had never lived with anyone. This was starting to get real.

Mae, seemingly satisfied with his sudden silence and furrowed brow, stood and grabbed her purse. She made her way toward the door.

"See you soon, *hubby*," she said as she shut the door behind her.

Chapter 10

Mae

Mae couldn't hide the smile on her face. She was the one who finally took Jonas off guard. The look on his face when she said she would be moving in was priceless. Why was he so shocked? He was the one who put this term in the agreement, which obviously made sense. If their fake marriage was to look real, then they had to make it look convincing.

Putting her parents' house on the market was bittersweet. It was where all her memories lived from when they were all together, happy as a family. She knew her parents would understand. They would be happy for her and Nico to be moving on and leaving the past behind them. Deep down, she was happy. The memories were nice, but they also made her sad. She could sometimes swear she smelled her mom's cinnamon rolls wafting up from the kitchen or hear her dad's old sports radio in the living room.

As much as she had come to terms with selling the house, there was still Nico to convince. The house had been left to both of them, and she wasn't sure he would be on board. When he came home from practice the next night, she had his favorite dinner on the table.

"Mmm. Spaghetti Bolognese," said Nico as he walked in the door and breathed in the delicious smells of tomato and garlic. "What's the occasion, sis?"

"Can't I just make my brother a meal he loves?"

"I guess." Nico eyed her skeptically as he put his sports duffel down in the entryway. He headed to the kitchen to wash his hands as she poured two glasses of malbec. She placed the glasses on the table and took a seat, trying to keep her nervousness at bay. Nico took the seat across from her. She held up her wine glass.

"Cheers."

"What are we cheersing to?" he asked, picking up his wine glass and holding it in the air close to hers.

"I don't know. To new beginnings," she said with a shrug.

"New beginnings, huh?"

They clinked glasses. Nico looked at her curiously, but she wouldn't meet his gaze. She began twirling spaghetti around her fork and took a big bite. She watched her brother scarf down his meal and fill his plate with seconds. "This is delicious, Mae," he said.

She nodded. "So, Nico. I've been thinking…"

"Mhmm," he said with his mouthful.

"You know I love you and we've been looking out for each other since Mom and Dad passed."

"Yes," he said, almost as a question.

"Well, don't you think it's time to be on your own? Don't get me wrong. I love living with you. I just think you're old enough to not live with your big sister anymore."

"But I like living with you. Who is going to cook for me?"

She rolled her eyes.

"I know, but I think you should be on your own. Spread your wings, as they say. It's not like you can't afford it."

"So, you want me to move out?" he asked, putting his fork down and eyeing her.

"Not necessarily. I want us both to move out."

"But this is Mom and Dad's house…"

"Don't you think it's time we move on? They'd want us to. You know that."

Nico nodded solemnly. "I still hear them sometimes, you know. Their laughter through the walls. There are so many memories here."

Mae felt her eyes tearing up. She and Nico didn't talk much about their parents. It was too sad a topic. "I hear them, too."

Nico took a deep breath. "Are you sure this is what you want?"

Mae nodded. "I'm sure. That is, if you're okay with it."

"Yeah, you're probably right, anyway. It's time to move on. It will be nice not having a babysitter anymore," he said with a wink.

They finished their dinner while talking about their parents and their favorite moments growing up. It was almost like they were saying their goodbyes right then. Once the dishes were washed and dried, Mae gave her brother a hug. "Thank you," she said softly.

"No, thank *you*, sis." Nico gave her a squeeze. "For everything." As he pulled away, she saw him wipe away a tear from his eye. "I better move out soon. You're turning me into a sap."

She laughed. "Do you have any idea where you want to live?"

"Yeah, a few players are looking for roommates. Could be fun."

She nodded and headed out of the kitchen and upstairs to her bedroom.

"I'll call the realtor tomorrow," she said, calling down the stairs.

The conversation with Nico had gone better than she expected. The realtor was eager to put the house on the market right away, since it was in a popular suburb near the city. Now, she had just signed an agreement to marry Jonas. She had already asked Braydon earlier that day for an unheard-of number of days off so she could pack up the house. After a moment of panic, he granted her the time off and thankfully, didn't ask too many questions. She just said that she was moving out of her childhood home. She didn't dare mention anything about Jonas yet. Nico didn't know either. She wasn't the best at keeping secrets, so she thought it better to say as little as possible to the people who knew her best.

No one could ever know that their marriage was a fake. She wouldn't be able to live it down. Instead, she would carry on like it was real and then get a fake divorce in a few years. Who knew? Maybe she and Jonas would look back and laugh about this whole thing. One thing she knew for sure was that she had to keep her emotions in check. She refused to let old feelings for Jonas resurface, no matter how close they got.

In the following days, Mae boxed up everything in her house. Nico helped where he could between practice and games. He kept telling her she should hire movers to help, but she wanted to do this on her own. It was a big deal, saying goodbye to this house. She'd only call movers when the truck needed to be loaded up.

"Are you sure you don't want any of this furniture?" asked Nico, as he was carrying an armchair downstairs.

"No. The place I'm moving into is actually furnished," she said, which wasn't a total lie.

"You still haven't told me where you're moving."

"It's a condo in the city. I'll have you come over once I'm all settled." Still, not a total lie, but she couldn't help but feel guilty for telling half-truths. She continued packing up the essentials that she would need for Jonas's. Okay, maybe she was packing a little more than *essentials,* just to mess with him.

When she had the movers carry her boxes into his condo, she watched from the doorway as his eyes widened. She could tell he was internally freaking out, which made her smile. She took a step inside and her breath caught as she glanced around the condo. It was beautiful. He had moved in a year ago, and this was her first time seeing it. It was on the top floor with floor-to-ceiling windows and an almost 360-degree view of the city down below.

"What do you think?" asked Jonas, stepping over the moving boxes toward her. He was wearing grey sweats and a white tee. She stared a beat too long. How could he look *that* good in sweats?

"It's nice," she said, pulling herself together. She didn't want him to see that she was impressed with his condo or him.

He nodded. "Would you like me to show you to your room?"

"It's not yours, is it?"

"No. Don't worry, Mae."

He motioned down a hallway. "This way."

She followed behind him with her suitcase. The concrete walls didn't have much on them besides a few pieces of modern art. He was very minimal, and here she was about to add clutter. She would enjoy this. The small annoyances would make him regret this agreement.

"Here we are," he said, opening the door.

The room was huge with more floor-to-ceiling windows and white, sheer curtains that hung lushly and kissed the floor. The bed was plush and sat on a creamy tufted bedframe. On either side were mirrored nightstands with dimly lit glass lamps.

"Wow," she said, not able to contain her admiration. "This is beautiful."

"I'm glad you like it," said Jonas.

"Was this always a guest room?"

"Yesterday it was a gym. My designer and I worked on it all morning."

She looked up at Jonas and their eyes caught. She felt her heart flutter. He did this for her. But why?

As if hearing her thoughts. "I wanted you to feel comfortable," he said softly.

"Thank you," she said. This was the Jonas she knew. Suddenly, she remembered her pact with herself to not let her feelings resurface. She shook her head slightly, as if to break the spell.

"Well, I better get settled," she said, laying her suitcase on the floor.

"Right. Well, I'm going to head to the office for a bit. But I'll see you later."

"Do whatever you want," she said with a shrug, looking through her suitcase.

Jonas nodded and headed out of the room, closing the door gently behind him. She stood and pressed her ear to the door. When she heard him walk out the front door and his keys in the lock, she let out a breath. She kicked off her shoes and faceplanted into the bed. This was a dream. Or was it? She was living with a man who she used to love, but was only here because it was convenient for him. She rolled onto her back and sighed. She could at least enjoy herself a little bit.

After unpacking her boxes, she made herself at home. As much as she could. Mae ordered groceries and put her favorite snacks in the pantry. She unpacked her toiletries and makeup, and organized them in the spacious bathroom connected to her room. When she felt settled, she drew a bath in the large white tub, poured some bubble bath in, and let her clothes fall to the marble floor. She stepped in and submerged herself under the water. It felt heavenly. She had been packing for three days straight.

As strange as it was to be in a new place, Mae felt surprisingly comfortable. She leaned her head back against the tub and looked up at the chandelier above. Had Jonas had the bathroom redesigned, too? This was way too feminine compared to the rest of the house. He couldn't be *that* nice. She shut her eyes and let herself relax.

A few moments later, she heard the front door unlock.

"I'm home," she heard Jonas call out. Her eyes snapped open.

Why is he announcing himself? Mae thought with a little laugh. He was acting like they were actually married. And that she actually cared when he came and went. She ignored him and shut her eyes again.

Suddenly, she heard the bathroom door open slowly. "Mae?"

Jonas stood in the doorway, oblivious. She sat up and covered herself in bubbles.

"Oh, my God. Do you knock?" she yelled.

His eyes shot to the tub where she sat holding herself. "Oh shit, I'm sorry," he said, covering his eyes. He still stood in the doorway.

"Get out!" she said, splashing water at him.

"Right, sorry," he said, walking into the doorframe before quickly shutting the door behind him.

Mae covered her mouth and stifled a laugh. This living arrangement was going to take some getting used to. For the both of them.

Chapter 11

Jonas

Jonas opened the dark-stained cabinet and pulled out a black mug, placing it on the counter with a clink. He poured himself a steaming cup of coffee from the carafe and took a sip, leaning against the counter. The warmth ran down his throat. The sound of slow footsteps entered the kitchen, joined shortly thereafter by the cabinets being opened and shut. Mae looked lost. She had been here for a few days and was still learning her way around.

After watching her for a moment, he tried to hide a smile as she stood on her tippy toes looking through the top cabinets. He let his eyes stray down to where her oversized shirt inched up teasingly. Jonas shook his head slightly and looked down into his cup of coffee. He couldn't let any feelings emerge, no matter how tempting.

Truthfully, at times it was hard to feel any temptation with Mae. She was so up and down with her moods, Jonas had whiplash trying to keep up. In ways, she was the same Mae he remembered. Grumpy before coffee. Witty. Beautiful. But she was also different from the Mae he remembered. How could he expect her not to be? They weren't the same people they used to be. They weren't together.

He watched as she moved around glasses and listened to her huff.

"Need some help?" Jonas smirked.

She turned to him with groggy eyes. "Where the hell are the coffee mugs?"

Jonas pointed above his head. "I put them above the coffeemaker. It's the logical choice."

Mae rolled her eyes and tried pushing him aside, but Jonas didn't budge. He took another sip of his coffee, smiling to himself.

"Are you always this annoying?" Mae asked, trying to reach the cabinet.

"Are you always this grumpy?"

She shot him a look.

"Okay, okay." He put his hands up and slid away from the cabinet.

She reached up, grabbed a mug, and poured herself a generous serving of coffee. She took a sip and let out an appreciative sigh. She eyed Jonas out of the corner of her eye.

"How long have you been up?" she asked sleepily.

"About an hour now."

"Ugh. Still an early bird. I don't know how you do it." She shook her head before taking another sip.

"I like the quiet of the morning. The city isn't quite awake yet." He looked out toward the clear views of the city.

She nodded and followed his gaze. "It *is* beautiful."

Jonas couldn't help thinking the same thing about her as she walked her cup of coffee to the window. Her hair fell in messy waves and her long legs moved gracefully. It wasn't like he had forgotten her beauty. He still saw her every day at the office, but seeing her in suits was much different from seeing her first thing in the morning.

They weren't sleeping in the same bed. Obviously. She mostly avoided going near him. But still, these mornings felt intimate. Familiar in a way. As grumpy as she was when she rolled out of bed, he enjoyed the company. It was a nice change from being alone. These little glimpses of her brought up a lot of memories, and it was hard for Jonas to push them away.

"It almost feels lonely," Mae said softly, breaking Jonas out of his thoughts.

"Hmm?" He looked at her.

"Being up here in this big home, looking over a city full of people." She didn't meet his gaze.

"Sometimes." Jonas said honestly.

They stood in silence, looking out over the city as the lights began to lose their luster with the sun rising. They watched the sky change from gray to purple to pink to blue. It was comfortable. It was like time stood still.

"Well, I better get ready for work," Mae said, finishing the last sip of coffee. She walked back to the kitchen and placed her mug in the sink before heading down the hallway to the bathroom. He heard the door shut and the shower turn on.

Jonas let out a sigh as if he had been holding his breath. He walked to the kitchen and placed his mug next to hers. Something so simple as two mugs in the sink made him smile. What was wrong with him? Maybe he had misjudged how difficult this would be. He shook it off and headed to his room.

As he got ready for work, he gave himself an internal pep talk. He had to focus. The festival was this week. He and Wendy had been planning it for months. It was their largest charity event of the year, and it needed to be perfect. Plus, he was about to embark on a huge partnership with Nate.

His dream partnership. The one thing that would separate him from who his father was. The one thing besides this marriage to Mae. Which, now that he thought of it, he made a mental note to go to his jeweler after work. He had to pick out their rings.

Jonas straightened out his suit before shutting his bedroom door behind him. He looked around the condo, but didn't see Mae. He wasn't about to look for her to say goodbye after he had walked in on her in the bathroom her first day here. He couldn't shake the mental snapshot he took of her soaked in bubbles. Instead, Jonas headed out the front door, locking it behind him.

Downstairs, his driver waited by the curb. He opened the door for Jonas, handing him the morning paper. Jonas slid into the backseat and turned the pages of the paper distractedly. Soon, they were at the office. Jonas was always the first one there. He entered his office and tried to focus on the workday ahead. The day went by in a slow blur, and only sped up when he saw Mae. It almost felt like it was years back when they were keeping their relationship a secret. It was exciting.

In the late afternoon, Jonas checked his watch. It was one o'clock. He let out a sigh. He usually didn't leave work early. In fact, it was quite the opposite. But today, his head just wasn't here. Plus, there was a game tonight. No one would question it. He grabbed his briefcase and called his driver.

"Where to, Mr. Matthews?" his driver asked as he opened the car door.

"Lieberman's."

Lieberman's was the best jeweler in the city. It was by appointment only, but they always made an exception for Jonas. Although, he usually only went around the holidays to pick out a gift for his mother.

The car pulled up to the glass building nestled between two large high rises. Jonas had been here several times, but for some reason he was nervous this time. He announced himself to the two security guards at the door who led him inside. Glass cases of sparkling jewelry sat on plush maroon floors. A large, crystal chandelier hung from the center of the room, directly under a large skylight, which made stars of light move elegantly across the walls.

"Mr. Matthews. What a pleasant surprise. We weren't expecting you today," said a short woman with a black bob cut. She approached him with her hands held out. Jonas offered his hand and she shook it graciously.

111

"Nice to see you, Elenore."

"What can we do for you today?" she asked curiously.

Jonas cleared his throat. "I'm here to look at engagement rings and wedding bands."

She raised her eyebrows in surprise. "Mr. Matthews. This is news to me. Usually, I know about every high-profile engagement in this city."

"Yes, well, this has been a private affair. I know I can trust your discretion."

"Of course." She nodded assuredly, trying to brush off her surprise. "Right this way."

She led him to a large glass case housing several settings. Jonas spent the next few hours looking at various combinations of settings and carats. Despite the marriage being a sham, he still felt the need to find the perfect ring for Mae. In fact, he had fun pulling different rings from their plush velvet holders.

Once he made his selection, Elenore carefully boxed the bands and engagement ring separately in matte navy-blue boxes. She tied the boxes with a white silk ribbon before placing them carefully in a bag.

"Whoever she is, she is a lucky woman," Elenore said, handing Jonas the bag.

Jonas nodded. "Thank you for all of your help."

Back at his condo, he placed the bag in the back of his closet. He would give her the rings tonight after the game. Jonas tried imagining her face and hoped it would be one of happiness. He checked his watch. It was already time to head to the game. He changed out of his suit and into a pair of jeans, a white shirt, and a baseball cap.

In the owner's box, he was one of the last to arrive.

"Nice of you to show up." Braydon called out when Jonas walked through the door.

Jonas shook his head at him and greeted everyone. He ordered a beer from the bar and casually looked around the room for Mae. He spotted her sitting in the front row, waiting intently for the game to begin. He felt nervous thinking about tonight. It was hard to focus on the game, but he followed everyone's lead and cheered when he needed to.

It ended up being a shutout. The owner's box became a full-on party. Music pumped through the speakers and drinks flowed. Jonas was happy for the win, but he was impatiently wanting to get home with Mae. He slipped his phone out of his pocket and texted her: *Want to get out of here?*

He watched her pull her phone from her pocket and read the notification. She glanced at him quickly with a look of curiosity. She gave a little nod as Braydon drunkenly started yelling the team chant. Jonas held back a smile and began saying his goodbyes. Everyone was too busy celebrating to care.

On the drive back to his condo, he couldn't keep his leg from shaking. He was nervous. Going to his closet, he dug the rings out of the bag and placed them in his back pocket. He pulled out a bottle of champagne and placed it in a bucket of ice on the coffee table. Then he waited. He paced his living room before taking a seat on the couch. After about an hour, he heard the key in the lock. Mae walked in, looking around hesitantly. Jonas stood from the couch.

"I didn't think you were coming," he said.

"You know how Braydon is. He did not want the party to end. Plus, I didn't want it to look fishy with us both leaving at the same time." She shrugged.

Jonas nodded.

"So, what's up?" she asked, curiously. She stood near the doorway, keeping her distance.

"I thought we could celebrate." Jonas said, gesturing to the champagne.

She looked at him suspiciously before giving a shrug of defeat. She walked toward him and took a seat on the couch. He sat next to her and gently removed the cork, hearing the pop and fizz. He shakily poured two glasses. Jonas could feel her watching him. He handed her the glass. They clinked their glasses together and took a sip.

It was now or never.

"So, I got you something," he said, reaching into his back pocket. He pulled out the ring box and heard her suck in a breath.

"Jonas." She looked up at the box and up at him. A flicker of happiness crossed her face and faded just as quickly. It was almost real for a moment. He gently took her hand, which was shaking slightly. That simple touch sent a shockwave through him. Shaky himself, he carefully slid the rings on her finger.

Chapter 12

Mae

The next day in the office, Mae sat at her desk, holding her hand in front of her face. It still hadn't hit her that she was engaged. No, *married*. Of course, it wasn't real. She somehow had to keep reminding herself of that every now and again, but this ring was *real*. All ten carats of it. The solitaire emerald-cut stone was set in a simple gold band, and cast a hundred flashes of light around her office. Jonas did well. If she didn't know any better, she would have thought he picked them out himself. But he had people for that.

Still, when he placed the rings on her finger last night, she couldn't help but feel something between them. It was his silent, almost nervous composure. The slight shake of his hands as he held hers that sent warmth through her whole body. There was a stillness in the room, as if time had momentarily stopped just for them.

"Jonas. This is too much," she had said, staring at the ring as it gently rested on the hand in her lap.

He shrugged modestly. She admired the ring a moment longer before holding out her hand expectantly.

"What?" Jonas raised his eyebrows.

"It's your turn. Give me your ring."

He slid his hand into his back pocket and handed her a small velvet box. Maybe it was the champagne or getting caught up in the moment, but Mae got on her knee and opened the box. Jonas let out a laugh and shook his head.

"Jonas Lee Matthews. Will you marry me for *all* the wrong reasons?" she asked, batting her eyelashes.

"I would love nothing more," he said, holding back a laugh. Mae slid the simple gold band on his finger and pulled herself up onto the couch. They poured two more glasses of champagne and celebrated this outrageous plan that, for a moment, felt real. It almost felt like it did all those years ago.

There was a knock at Mae's door, pulling her from the memory of last night, and she abruptly lowered her hand and opened her laptop, trying to look busy. "Come in," she called out.

The door opened and Braydon stepped in. He was the last person she wanted to see right now. How was she going to hide the giant ring on her finger? They hadn't announced their engagement to anyone yet. Jonas wanted to wait until the charity festival, but insisted they wear their rings so their story panned out. Still, Mae wasn't prepared to answer questions, especially from her nosy boss.

"Hi, Braydon," she said, a little too enthusiastically.

He gave her a look before gesturing to the chair across from her desk.

"Yes, please. Sit, sit." Mae nodded.

"I was hoping we could talk about the upcoming festival." Braydon eased himself into the chair.

"Sure," Mae said, placing her hands on her lap and out of sight. How in the world was she supposed to keep this up?

"Can you pull up the guest list for the chairmen?" Braydon nodded toward her laptop.

"Mhmm." She angled the laptop in front of her and began nervously opening documents. "Here it is."

She turned the laptop quickly to face Braydon and covered her left hand. But not quickly enough.

"What is that?" Braydon eyed her hands.

"Hmm?"

"That. The huge diamond that just momentarily blinded me."

Mae felt panic run through her, leaving her speechless. She should have been more prepared for this.

"Mae! Did you get engaged?" Braydon asked, his voice rising.

She nodded slowly and gave him a nervous smile. "Married, actually."

"When? How? Who?" Braydon stood from his seat excitedly.

"Calm down. Before you give yourself a heart attack," she said with a laugh.

Braydon scoffed and placed his hands on her desk, leaning in. "Tell me everything."

"Well, we really haven't told anyone yet."

"Is it someone I know?"

"You could say that." Mae fidgeted in her chair, avoiding Braydon's questioning gaze.

"That's a looker of a ring. It's either a seasoned player or a CEO." He eyed the ring, calculating in his head.

He continued making guesses, until Mae blurted out, "It's Jonas."

"Jonas?" Braydon nearly choked.

Mae nodded.

"Since when?"

"We've been together for a while. We just weren't ready to come out yet, but then he proposed, and we decided to elope."

"So, *that's* why you took that weekend off…" Braydon nodded his head, piecing everything together.

"Yes, but please, Braydon. No one knows yet. Please don't say anything."

Braydon nodded. "I'll have to tell Julia."

Mae rolled her eyes. "Fine."

Julia was Braydon's wife, and she knew if Braydon couldn't tell anyone he would drive himself crazy.

"Great. Let's all go to dinner tonight then," Braydon said, slapping her desk with his palm.

"I don't know—" Mae said hesitantly.

"Nonsense. We have to celebrate, and I want to hear *everything*." He started for the door.

"But what about the guest list?" she called after him.

He waved her off with a grin. "We'll get to it later. There are more important things at hand."

120

That night, Mae stood before the bathroom mirror, applying lipstick. She smoothed her hair into a low ponytail and secured it with an elastic. She turned and looked over her shoulder at her reflection. Her silk emerald green dress draped low in the back as she tied it at the neck. She had bought it after work. Braydon insisted she leave early to shop for the occasion. When Mae saw this dress in the shop window, she immediately thought of Jonas.

"I can't believe you agreed to dinner," she heard him call from the living room.

"You really expect me to be able to hide this ring?" she said, walking out of the bathroom. She spotted Jonas leaning casually against the couch in an all-black suit. His hair was still damp from the shower. For a second, her breath caught.

"Plus, there's no game tonight. There was no way out of it," she said as she entered the living room. When Jonas saw her, he straightened and cleared his throat nervously. She smiled.

"You look…" he paused, as if trying to find the right word. "You look good."

"Thank you," she said quietly, willing him to say what he really felt.

"Well, we should go." He gestured toward the door.

Disappointed, she slid past him as he held the door open for her. She could feel his eyes on her back, and it gave her a hint of happiness. She still had an effect on him.

When they got to the restaurant, the hostess informed them that Braydon and Julia were already at the table waiting for them. Jonas stepped closer and placed his hand on the small of her back. Although his hand was warm, she shivered at his touch. She looked up at him nervously.

"You ready for this?" he whispered.

She nodded.

He led her through the restaurant, following the hostess. As they approached the table, Braydon stood, giving them both hugs. Julia did, too. They all sat down and a waiter appeared with a bottle of champagne on ice.

"Our finest champagne, sir."

"Thank you. Only the best for our newlyweds." Braydon winked at Jonas and Mae.

The waiter poured four glasses and quickly took their orders.

"Congratulations to the happy couple," Julia said, holding up her glass.

Jonas put his arm around Mae and pulled her close, as the four of them clinked their glasses.

She felt stiff being this close to him, but he seemed completely comfortable. His fingers grazed her arm softly as he took a sip of champagne. She took a generous sip of hers to help loosen her nerves.

"So, how did this come about?" Julia asked, pointing at the two of them.

"Yes, please. Do tell," Braydon said, nodding.

"Well, I've always had my eye on this one." Jonas nodded toward Mae. "How could I not? She's beautiful."

Julia was practically already gushing.

"But she didn't make it easy on me," Jonas continued. "She's a stubborn one."

"Don't I know it," Braydon said with a laugh.

Mae playfully rolled her eyes and took another sip of champagne.

"But eventually, she finally agreed to go on a date with me," Jonas said, giving her a squeeze. This was her cue.

"Yes, I finally broke. It was the sweetest thing. He set up a late-night picnic in his living room, with the fireplace crackling, and a nice bottle of wine," she said, remembering the night because it had happened.

"How romantic." Julia sighed.

Jonas looked at Mae and caught her gaze. "I remember looking at her in the glow of the fireplace, and thinking, *I can't let this one go.*"

Something about the way he said it made Mae's stomach do a small flip. His eyes told her he was telling the truth. She looked at his lips and brought her hands to his face, bringing him in for a soft kiss. She felt Jonas take in a breath as his lips met hers for that brief moment. She pulled back and looked at him. His eyes slowly opened and they beamed. She laid her head on his shoulder, watching Braydon and Julia gush over them. The champagne had definitely gone to her head.

Jonas stumbled over his words for a moment before collecting himself. "So yeah, now we're married."

"Cheers to that!" Braydon said.

The rest of the dinner went smoothly. Between the two of them, Mae and Jonas had enough real memories to really sell their relationship. Braydon was eating it all up. By the end of dinner, he was hugging Jonas, which was a sight Mae never thought she would see.

"My boy, you two really kept this under wraps, but I'm glad to see the both of you settled." He slapped Jonas on the back. Jonas smiled proudly.

Braydon gave Mae a big hug as well, and discreetly slipped her a check before whispering in her ear. "Buy the pair of you something ridiculous." He walked away, hand in hand with Julia, before she could protest.

"Well, that went well." Jonas let out a sigh of relief as he slid his arm around Mae's bare shoulders. She looked at him curiously. Wasn't their little show over? He must have seen the look on her face because he cleared his throat and removed his arm.

"I'll call my driver." He pulled out his phone.

They rode home in silence and on opposite ends of the seat. It was as if some spell had been broken and they were back to normal. Mae didn't like it. Why had she let herself kiss him? That had been a mistake. As much as she was fighting them back, her feelings were coming to the surface.

"Home sweet home," Jonas said, kicking off his shoes as they walked through the door.

But it's not my home, Mae reminded herself as she pulled the check from her clutch. She waited until Jonas was in the kitchen to unfold it. When she did, she nearly choked. It was a check for $500,000.

"Are you okay?" Jonas asked, walking toward her. For a second, she debated showing him, but she wasn't selfish.

"Yeah. Braydon gave us a gift. An outrageous one," she said, holding out the check.

Jonas took it from her hands and read the amount. He raised his eyebrows.

"Wow. Maybe he doesn't hate me after all. This really is working."

Mae nodded slowly.

"Keep it." He handed her back the check.

"What?" she asked, shocked.

"It's not like I need it." He turned toward his bedroom and started to walk away.

Mae stood still, holding the check and looking after him.

"Good job tonight, by the way. That kiss really sold them," he called over his shoulder.

Mae swore she felt her heart crack.

Chapter 13

Jonas

Jonas put the key in the lock of his front door and walked inside. Immediately, he was hit with a delicious aroma coming from the kitchen. Roasted garlic and simmering tomatoes wafted in the air. He set his briefcase on the entryway table and loosened his tie. It had been a long day at the office and coming home to a home-cooked meal was everything he didn't know he needed.

"Mae?" he called out.

"In here!" she called from the kitchen, peeping around the corner with a little wave.

"It smells amazing in here."

"Oh good. I'm trying a new recipe." She held up a spoon and smiled.

Jonas looked her up and down quickly before she turned back to the stove. Her face was beautifully bare and her hair was up in a messy bun. She wore an old team shirt and shorts that barely grazed her upper thighs. In the two weeks she had been at his place, she had slowly become more and more comfortable in her new home.

Not just in how she dressed, but in how she was with Jonas.

Despite their history and this plan he had forced her into, Mae had somehow softened. He would catch glimpses of how she used to be. Of the girl he fell for. She had started spending less time holed up in her room and more time in the common areas of the condo.

He would find her curled up on the couch typing on her laptop, or by the fireplace reading a book. Lately, she started having dinner ready for him, whether she cooked it herself or ordered some of their old favorites. It felt nostalgic sitting at the kitchen counter eating Chinese food straight from the carton, or sipping chilled white wine while watching bad reality TV, or simply sitting in a comfortable silence. These were things he had missed.

This was the life they had before Jonas had screwed it up. This was the life they could have had if he had realigned his priorities. But he hadn't. He had chosen his work, and right now, he had to remind himself of that as he watched Mae cooking in his kitchen. Still, he enjoyed her company. He enjoyed coming home to a not empty condo for once. It almost felt like they were a real married couple.

"I'm going to hop in the shower," Jonas said after watching her for a moment from the living room.

"Okay. Dinner should be ready in twenty." She stirred a sauce simmering in the pan.

Jonas nodded and headed toward his bedroom, shutting the door behind him. He took a hot shower, watching the glass blur with fog. He stayed in a minute longer with the unrealistic thought Mae would step in and join him. He laughed to himself. She wasn't *that* comfortable, but he let his thoughts go there for a minute anyway.

It was beginning to get more and more difficult not to touch her. He found himself loving when Braydon was around. Something he thought he would never say. But it meant he could put his arm around Mae or place his hand on her lower back. Any chance he could touch her, he took. They hadn't kissed since the restaurant, but Jonas thought about it all the time. The way she had looked at him before she pressed her lips against his. He wanted to kiss her again, and not just because Braydon was watching.

Jonas sighed and turned off the water before stepping out and wrapping himself in a plush white towel. Another reminder of her. She had slowly integrated herself into his place. First it started with pots and pans filling his cabinets. Jonas never cooked for himself. He had delivery for dinner almost every night. She recorded shows on his TV that were hilariously bad, but he somehow got sucked in to. She lit candles that smelled of vanilla and warm spices. She bought new luxury towels and sheets, which she offered to him as a gift for her staying there. She was everywhere, and Jonas didn't mind it.

He dried off, slipped on some black joggers and a faded Henley tee, and walked to the kitchen.

"You're just in time," said Mae as she set silverware on the table. "Would you mind pouring some wine? I picked up a nice red after work."

"Sure." Jonas walked to the bar and pulled down a pair of wine glasses. He unscrewed the cork of the wine bottle and poured two generous servings.

"It's a Bolognese." She set a steaming bowl of pasta in front of Jonas as he took a seat at the table.

"It looks fantastic. I could get used to these home-cooked meals." He handed her the wine.

Mae gave him a smile that was almost sad. "Well, enjoy it. Maybe I could even teach you how

130

to cook a few simple dinners before—" she stopped and took a sip of wine.

Jonas stayed silent for a moment before changing the subject. "So, how was work today?"

"Good. Surprisingly slow, given the festival is so soon. Braydon is actually not driving himself or me crazy for nice," she said, taking a bite. "You were there late."

"Always."

"Some things never change." Mae shook her head.

"Oh, really?"

"Come on, Jonas. You live and breathe work."

"Not anymore," he lied.

Mae let out a laugh.

"I'll tell you what. Next week, I'll leave the office at five p.m. every day. Clock out when everyone else does."

"I'll believe it when I see it."

"Just you wait. You'll be sick of seeing me here so much."

She laughed. "Fine. It's a challenge."

The next week at the office, Jonas wondered why he had ever made the bet with Mae. He was stressed about getting everything done in an eight-hour day. It wasn't what he was used to, but he was determined to prove to Mae he could do it.

He didn't know why he had promised this to her. Maybe it was proving her wrong. Or maybe it was proving he could be a different man for her. Either way, it was taking a toll on him, and it was only Tuesday.

He heard a soft knock on the door as he sorted through paperwork.

"Come in." he barked.

"S-s-sorry, Mr. Matthews. You have a call on line one. I tried buzzing you."

Jonas glanced at the phone on his desk and saw the red light flashing. He ran his fingers through his hair and let out a sigh.

"I see it now. I'll take the call. Thank you, Wendy," he said, softening. He had unintentionally been taking his stress out on her. She had been avoiding him all day, slinking around the office quietly as not to disturb him.

"Of course." She quietly nodded and walked out, closing the door behind her.

He picked up the phone. "This is Jonas."

"Jonas. I was beginning to think you were avoiding me." He heard his mother's voice on the other line.

"Hi, Mother. I'm sorry. It's just been a madhouse at the office lately."

He heard her sigh. "And here I had my hopes up that a woman might be occupying your time. *That* I wouldn't mind."

Jonas let out a little laugh. Little did she know. He asked how Hawaii was and talked about the upcoming festival. Several times, he had the urge to tell her about Mae. He knew how happy she would be to know he had gotten married. So happy, she would probably even get over the fact that they eloped without anyone knowing. He decided against it, though. She would find out when everyone else did.

After he hung up with her, Jonas got back to the work on his desk. Only a few minutes had passed before his door swung open. *What now?* He looked up to see Nico storming in, and Wendy trailing behind him with wide eyes. Jonas stood up swiftly as he approached with a crazed look.

"Nico. What's this—"

Before Jonas could finish his sentence, Nico swung a punch. Wendy let out a small scream. Jonas swerved backward and Nico missed, causing him to stumble forward. He caught himself and stood face to face with Jonas, glowering.

"Swing at me again. Try it," Jonas said sternly.

Nico glared at him before backing away.

"Should I call someone, Mr. Matthews?" asked Wendy, her voice shaking.

"No, Wendy. It's quite all right. You can go," said Jonas calmly, waving his hand toward the door.

She gave a little nod and hesitantly backed out of the office, closing the door behind her. Jonas took a seat at his desk and folded his hands, looking at Nico, who was now pacing back and forth.

"If you pull anything like that again, I'll have you off the team," said Jonas. It wasn't entirely true. Even though he was the owner, there was a signed contract. But Nico didn't know that, and a quick flash of fear showed in his eyes.

"What are you doing with my sister? Breaking her heart before wasn't enough?" asked Nico, crossing his arms.

This caught Jonas off guard for a moment before he composed himself. "We eloped."

"You *what?*" Nico's voice rose.

"Yes. Your sister is now my wife." A casual smile crossed his lips as he shrugged.

Nico stood in shocked silence. Jonas could see the blood drain from his face. To Nico, this was a huge betrayal from the person he trusted the most. Jonas felt guilt creep in. Nico was Mae's brother, and she loved him very much. This was crushing him, which would only hurt Mae in the end.

"Look, I'm righting a wrong," said Jonas quietly.

"Ha. Somehow, I don't believe that."

"I care about her."

"You only care about yourself." Nico remained quiet before speaking again. "She deserves better. She'll realize that eventually."

Jonas knew this, but the words still cut through him. Nico was right.He straightened in his chair. "Don't you have conditioning?" he asked coolly.

Nico glared at him, but didn't budge.

"What are you still doing here? What am I paying you for?" Jonas crossed his arms.

Nico huffed before turning and leaving, slamming the door behind him.

Jonas let out a sigh and ran his fingers through his hair before holding his head in his hands. This was a mess. A mess he expected, but he didn't think it would affect him this much. He thought he would feel satisfaction in delivering the news to Nico, but he felt the opposite. This was going to hurt Mae, and that was the last thing he wanted.

How did Nico find out, anyway? Had Mae told him? Had Braydon? All these questions ran through his head. His phone rang, breaking him from his thoughts. He quickly picked it up, expecting it to be Mae with some explanation.

"Hello? Mae?" he asked, exasperated. He needed answers.

"Um, no. But maybe she would explain why I'm downstairs waiting for a meeting that should have started ten minutes ago," Nate said on the other line.

"Mr. Brockton." Jonas glanced at his watch and quickly stood from his desk. "I'll be right down."

He stormed out of his office and shot Wendy a look. She still looked shaken from the altercation she just witnessed.

"Why didn't you tell me Nate Brockton is downstairs?" he barked at Wendy.

"I'm so sorry, Mr. Matthews. I got so distracted by -"

He held up his hand, cutting her off, and walked swiftly past her as she called out more apologies.

In the elevator, he took a few deep breaths and smoothed his suit. Whatever had just happened with Nico would have to be shelved for another time. All his focus had to be on this meeting. He scolded himself for letting personal relations get in

the way of work. His father was probably laughing
in his grave.

Chapter 14

Mae

Mae sat by the window, holding a hot cup of coffee between her hands. She looked out at the busy city street that was slicked with morning rain. Breathing in the steam coming up from her cup, she took a sip. The sounds of the coffee shop were nosy but comforting. This was her favorite spot to come before work.

As much as she enjoyed being at Jonas's condo, which was surprising to her, she still loved having this place to come to. It was a little escape for her. An escape from seeing Jonas fresh out of the shower. An escape from smelling the sweetness of his cologne. An escape from him looking at her like he really wanted her.

Each day she had a harder and harder time pushing down her feelings. She was afraid she was going to burst and do something erratic. Like tell him how she felt, or grab him and kiss him. She shook her head. Why did she ever agree to this?

Her phone vibrated on the table. Nico. Again. She sighed. She had been avoiding him. It was becoming difficult to be around her brother when she was keeping this from him. She had never kept anything from him. The secret was getting harder to carry. She didn't know what would be worse, though. Keeping her marriage to Jonas under wraps, or seeing the look on her brother's face when he found out she was married to the one man he hated.

Maybe he would come around to Jonas. He did seem different. He had kept his promise of coming home on time, even though he did seem a little stressed last night. Mae tried to pry gently, but he just brushed off her questions. He had a meeting with Nate Brockton. Maybe it hadn't gone well.

As the evening went on, he eventually loosened up. They had ordered their favorite pizza and sat out on the patio, watching the sunset. She had felt so comfortable. So happy. It was hard not to get wrapped up in their charade. Was it even really a charade when no one was watching?

"I thought I'd find you here," she heard Nico's voice call out from behind her.

She spun around on her stool and looked at him, surprised. "Nico! What are you doing here?"

"I came to talk to you." He took the seat next to her.

"Okay?" She never saw her brother this serious.

"I know, Mae. I know everything."

She felt an unease in the pit of her stomach. She looked at him questioningly.

"When were you going to tell me you *married* Jonas?" He gave her a pointed look.

"What? How did you—" She shook her head, and covered the rings on her left hand.

"You can stop hiding the damn rings. I saw the diamond from the door of the coffee shop."

She looked down at her lap as he grabbed her hand gently. He studied the ring for a moment.

"So, it's true," he said quietly.

"I was going to tell you." She didn't meet his gaze.

"Why? Why him?"

"Why not?"

Nico let out a mean laugh. "Let me count the ways."

"Oh, like *you* have the best track record," she said defensively.

"I never actually went through with any of them. I didn't *marry* them."

"And that makes you any better? You never follow through with anything. At least I took a chance."

140

"On the worst guy ever."

"He's not like that." Mae shook her head.

"What? He's not a power-hungry asshole?"

"You don't know him."

"Then enlighten me."

"I don't need to explain anything to you."

"You're making a mistake, Mae. Well, actually you've already made it."

Mae shook her head. This hurt. Her brother was ashamed of her, and she was ashamed of herself. Sitting here defending Jonas, she realized she had let herself fall for him again, or maybe she had never stopped falling for him. She bit her lip as she blinked back tears.

Nico softened for a moment as he put his hands on her shoulders. "I just don't want you to get hurt. Again," he said softly.

"Again?" she asked curiously.

"You think I didn't know about before? I saw the way you two looked at each other. Plus, you were never home."

"I didn't know anyone knew."

"Yeah. And I knew he must have hurt you when you locked yourself in your room and cried for weeks."

Mae remained quiet.

"I didn't think you'd be so stupid again," said Nico.

She felt anger rise up. "Stupid? Really, Nico? Coming from the guy who is constantly getting in trouble and has his sister bail him out? Maybe I deserve to be a little reckless. My whole life I've spent taking care of you."

"Mae, I—"

"No. It's my turn to do whatever the hell I want. I'm done being your mother when I never asked to be."

She saw the hurt wash over Nico's face, but she didn't care. So many feelings were swirling around inside of her that she could barely think straight. She stood abruptly, grabbing her coffee and pastry bag of almond croissants.

"Now, if you don't mind, I have to go to work and see my *husband.*" She walked away, leaving Nico looking at her like a sad puppy dog.

At the office, the entire day she could hardly focus. Anger and sadness consumed her. She was thankful Jonas was in meetings all day because she couldn't bear to look at him when she felt like this. She somehow managed to get her work done. She could tell Braydon knew something was up, but thankfully he didn't ask questions. Just after five, she packed up her belongings and drove to Jonas's, her anger still stewing.

She walked through the door and was surprised to see Jonas sitting on the couch reading the paper with the fire blazing. Why did he have to choose today to follow through on his promise of being on time? He looked up at her and checked his watch.

"Well, look at that," he said playfully. "I beat you home."

"Oh, shut up," Mae snapped.

Jonas looked taken aback. "Okay. Rough day at work?"

"You could say that." Mae's voice shook.

"Mae. What is it?" Jonas stood from the couch and slowly stepped toward her.

She threw her purse on the entry table and glared at Jonas. "You told Nico about us."

"No. He already knew. I don't know how or—"

Mae held up her hand. "Why didn't you tell me?"

"I was going to. He stormed into my office yesterday and tried to fight me."

"What?" Mae covered her mouth with her hand.

"Yeah. That's why I was so worked up yesterday."

"I *asked* you what was wrong. You should have told me." Her voice rose.

Jonas nodded weakly. "I know."

"Nico confronted me this morning. It was awful. We both said horrible things."

"I'm sorry."

"You should have prepared me, Jonas. He's my brother!"

"He'll get over it." Jonas shrugged.

"He'll get *over* it?" Mae asked pointedly.

"He's a big boy. You really need to stop babying him."

She stepped closer to Jonas, who was now leaning casually against the couch. She hated the smug look on his face. Was he enjoying this? Was his plan all along just to hurt Nico? What sick game was he playing?

"I can't believe you," she said, jabbing a finger into his chest. He looked down at her and furrowed his brow. Mae glared up at him. They hadn't been this close outside of the watchful eyes of Braydon. She could hear him breathing as she waited expectantly. She wasn't sure what she was waiting for. An apology? An explanation? Something else?

Everything she was pushing down these past few weeks, years even, was at the surface and ready to explode. This was what she feared. She was going to do something erratic.

She lifted her hands and pushed him roughly into the back of the couch, taking him by surprise. Before he could do anything, her hands were in his hair, pulling his face toward hers. She closed her eyes and pressed her lips against his. They kissed for just a second before he pulled away. He pressed his forehead against hers and looked at her as if he were in pain from holding back.

"Mae," he whispered.

"Don't talk." She pulled him in and kissed him again, but this time he didn't pull away. Instead, his hands were on her back, pulling her against him. His tongue ran across her lips before parting them to massage against hers. She felt him breathe into her as the kiss went from rhythmic to desperate. She let out a quiet moan.

He pressed away from the back of the couch, still kissing her, and led her around to the front. He pushed her gently and her knees gave, making her fall onto the plush cream couch. He slowly lowered and knelt on the carpet, looking at her intently. She stared back at him as his hands moved slowly up her legs. He slid them under her dress, brushing her inner thighs as he parted them. Her breath became heavy as he rubbed his thumb across her panties, his gaze never breaking.

He moved against her slowly. The sensation of his thumb and the silky fabric was agonizing, but delicious. She watched him smile as he pulled the fabric to the side. He dipped a finger inside of her slowly before pulling it out.

He slid his finger inside her again, massaging her with his palm. She leaned her head back and closed her eyes. As his fingers slowly pulled out, she felt his warm breath against her. He pushed her dress above her hips and brushed his lips against her, causing her to shudder. He gently sucked before parting her with the warmth of his tongue. She grasped the couch desperately, to hold still as he flicked his tongue against her.

Mae arched her lower back, trying to get closer to him. As she grabbed his hair and pulled roughly, he climbed up her slowly. She could feel his erection through his pants. She pulled at his shirt, too impatient to work at the buttons. He pulled it over his head swiftly, revealing the hard muscles of his stomach. She slid her hands up his chest as he looked at her hungrily.

"I need you. Now," she whispered into his ear before running her tongue across his earlobe. She felt him shudder and then his hands were tugging at her dress, pulling it up over her head. His eyes took her in for a moment. She leaned against the couch and arched her chest toward him. He groaned as his hands moved rapidly to his belt buckle. He undid it and unbuttoned his pants, his erection just inches away from her.

Jonas grabbed her panties and pulled them down swiftly, tossing them to the floor. He gripped her hips and slid her down to the base of the couch. She looked at him coyly as she slowly spread her legs wider. He looked at her and shook his head.

"You don't know how long I've wanted to do this," he murmured.

"Do what?" she asked innocently, slowly reaching down and massaging him.

He shook his head and let her move her hand up and down his shaft. Mae felt Jonas throbbing in her hands, which only made her want him more. She slid down further and rubbed the tip of him against her wet opening. He groaned. She swirled around him teasingly, enjoying watching him squirm.

She watched as his eyes shot to hers intently. He grabbed her hands suddenly and held them above her head. She knew what was coming, but feeling him push into her still took her by surprise. She moaned in pleasure as he filled her and then slowly pulled out. Desperately, she grabbed his lower back and pushed him into her again. He let out a breath and pumped into her faster. Her insides were throbbing around him as she exploded into a million different pieces. He let out a groan as he came with her.

They were in trouble now.

Chapter 15

Jonas

Jonas sat at the kitchen island, sipping on coffee. He heard Mae stir on the couch and watched as she stretched and untangled herself from the blankets. They had definitely crossed a line last night. Twice, to be exact. It was better than he had remembered. It was heated, almost desperate. He knew he wanted to do it again, but wasn't sure what Mae was thinking.

Afterward, they hadn't said much. They'd simply lain in silence, intertwined on the couch with the blaze of the fire the only light. It felt comfortable. She was in no rush to get up, and neither was he. He watched as she had fallen asleep on his chest, where his heart beat calmly. He truly felt at home.

"Good morning," said Mae groggily from the couch.

"Morning."

He caught her eye and watched as she shyly wrapped herself in a knit blanket. She stood from the couch, carefully covering herself, and made her way to the kitchen.

"Coffee. Please," she said, nodding at the steaming pot.

Jonas nodded. "How did you sleep?"

"Good.   You?"

"Very good." Jonas poured her a cup of coffee and handed it to her. She avoided his gaze and took a slow sip.

He wanted to know how she felt about last night. He wanted to know if it would happen again. He wished it would. Clearing his throat, Jonas asked, "So, last night was... pretty amazing."

She remained quiet, so Jonas continued. "I didn't think we would ever do that again. I really missed—"

"Last night was a mistake, Jonas," she said quietly, looking into her cup of coffee.

He felt his heart drop. "But I thought you wanted... You were the one who—"

"It was a temporary lapse of judgment. My head was out of sorts. Everything with this fake marriage, and Nico, and work. I wasn't thinking."

"Why does there have to be any thinking involved? We were in the moment, and it was a damn good moment."

"Well, it can't happen again." She finally looked up at him. "It will only complicate things. You wanted a fake wife, not a real one."

Jonas nodded. He thought about her words. She was right. This whole arrangement was strictly for business. He didn't want a real marriage with a white picket fence in the suburbs, although the image of sharing that life with Mae popped into his head. It wasn't a bad one. No. He couldn't let his feelings get away from him.

"You're right," said Jonas. "Besides, I need my head on straight if I'm to get into business with Nate. There's no room for anything else."

Mae pressed her lips together in a grim smile and nodded. "Exactly."

"Well, I better get ready for work." Jonas grabbed his cup of coffee and walked to his bedroom, leaving Mae alone in the kitchen.

In the office, Jonas was all smiles. Despite Mae putting an end to things, he couldn't stop thinking about their night together.

"Good morning, Wendy. You're looking nice today," he said, stopping at his secretary's desk. He placed a cup of coffee in front of her. "I brought you your favorite from that café up the street."

Wendy looked at him, a little dumbfounded. "Erm, thank you. This is unexpected."

Jonas gave her a little smile and a shrug.

"Is everything okay?" She raised an eyebrow at him.

"More than okay."

"You seem very…chipper today. Did something happen last night?" she pried.

"Can't a man just be in a good mood?" He smiled at her.

"It's just the other night was—"

"Oh, that was nothing. Boys will be boys." Jonas waved her off.

"It seemed a little intense. I was worried," said Wendy slowly.

"You worry too much. Enjoy your coffee." Jonas winked at her and headed into his office.

At his desk, he did his usual morning routine of checking his digital calendar and going through his emails. He caught sight of Mae walking by his office. She wore a cream-colored suit and her hair was pulled into a low bun. The scent of her lingered on his skin. She avoided looking his direction and continued moving.

Jonas frowned. How could she so easily turn her feelings off? He knew last night was just as intense for her as it was for him. That fire had always been there between them, and last night it ran rampant. He needed it to happen again. He needed her again. All of her.

Wendy knocked lightly at his door.

"Come in, come in!" He waved her in, smiling.

She looked cautiously around as if Nico was going to pop out of a corner and start swinging.

"I just forwarded you an email. It's from Mr. Brockton. After I dropped the ball the other night, I wanted to make sure I told you right away."

"Thank you, Wendy. I'll get to it right now."

She nodded and walked out, closing the door behind her. Jonas opened his inbox and clicked on the email. He read it excitedly and let out a "Whoop!"

The design team he was set on for his athletic line had agreed to take him on as a client, as long as Nate was behind the manufacturing team. They were the only team Jonas had his eye on and he had been intent on cutting a deal. After the rocky start to his meeting with Nate the other day, he was surprised to see things moving forward.

He buzzed Wendy from his phone. "Get in here, Wendy!"

She was at his door within seconds. "Yes, sir?"

He got up from his desk and hugged her, swinging her around. "We did it! We got the deal!" he cried.

"That's amazing! Congratulations!" Wendy laughed and tried to find her footing.

"Let's celebrate! Champagne!" Jonas clapped.

"It's only ten a.m." Wendy checked her watch.

"Just a little bit!" Jonas was already pulling a champagne bottle from the wine fridge under the bar.

"What has gotten into you?" Wendy laughed.

"I don't know, but I like it." Jonas said, knowing full well what it was. *Who* it was.

They toasted to the new partnership and for the next hour began going over the party details for the festival. Wendy had already hired all of the caterers and designated the design teams. It should go off without a hitch.

"Now, I want you to call Delaney's and order the entire office lunch on me," said Jonas.

"You've got it, boss." Wendy gave a little salute before heading back to her desk.

"Send an email to everyone to meet in the conference room in an hour," he called after her.

At lunchtime, everyone gathered in the conference room. It was very rare when everyone would eat lunch together like this. It was usually only around the holidays, so everyone was surprised to walk into a full spread on the table. There was prime rib, mashed potatoes, sautéed green beans, cherry pie, and a few bottles of red wine.

"What's the occasion?" asked Braydon as he walked in.

"Just thought we could all use a break over some good food." Jonas said, patting him on the back.

"You're awfully chipper. Married life suits you," he whispered, nudging Jonas in the arm.

"You may be right about that," said Jonas, just as Mae walked in the room. She looked around, confused for a moment, before catching Jonas's eye.

"Wow, Mr. Matthews. This is some spread," she said, as she walked past him to grab a plate.

"It must be torture not being able to be with her," whispered Braydon.

"Hmm?" Jonas momentarily thought the old man could read his mind.

"I, for one, can't wait until you announce it. I'm no good at secrets. I'm surprised I've held out this long."

Jonas nodded. "Soon enough."

The office staff enjoyed a long lunch together. It almost felt like a Thanksgiving feast, and everyone groaned when it was over because they had to get back to work. Throughout lunch, Jonas would notice Mae looking at him every so often. Her gaze was unreadable, but he was just happy to have those small moments of attention. Was she thinking about last night, too?

When everyone had cleared the conference room, Jonas helped Wendy clean up. After, he headed down to the gym to check in on conditioning. Normally, he didn't check in with the team unless it was game day. But he knew Nico would be there and he wanted to make his presence as the boss known. The incident in his office could not happen again.

The elevator doors opened to the large gym, and there were hushed whispers as Jonas stepped into the room. The team was spread across the floor with the various trainers. Some were lifting weights, others were doing calisthenics drills, and a group was running on the treadmills.

"Jonas! What brings you down here?" Chad called out as he placed his weights on the rack before making his way over.

Jonas noticed Nico shoot him a glance from across the gym floor. "Just checking in on how things are going down here. Can't have you boys getting soft on me."

"Soft? Never." Chad flexed his arms and puffed his chest.

Jonas let out a laugh. "Get back to work. Pretend I'm not here."

Chad nodded and jogged back to the weight rack as Jonas made his rounds and greeted the players. He made sure to smile extra wide and make cheerful banter with everyone because he could feel Nico's eyes on him. He wanted him to know that he was happy. He wanted him to believe it was because of Mae, which it was.

"Hey, boss," said Nico as Jonas approached. He was foam-rolling on one of the large mats with his trainer.

"Nico. Nice to see you." Jonas nodded before turning to the trainer.

"How are his stats, Joe?" asked Jonas. He didn't really care. It was just for show. He wanted Nico to feel nervous, and it worked.

"He's looking good, Mr. Matthews. We are about to work on his pitches."

"Good, good. If he wants to start at the next game, we need him in tip-top shape."

Nico shot him a nervous look. "I'll be good, boss."

"Carry on." Jonas nodded.

He smiled to himself as he walked toward the elevators to leave. That was just the reminder Nico needed to know who was in charge. Back in his office, Jonas could hardly concentrate on work. Memories of the night before kept interrupting his thoughts. Mae's hands on him. His lips on her. The sound of her breathing as they lost control together. He ran his fingers through his hair and let out a long sigh. He glanced at his watch. It was five o'clock. Time to head home.

As he walked down to his car, he gave himself a pat on the back for keeping his promise to Mae. He had left work on time every day this week. He thought he should celebrate. He had his driver drop him at Mae's favorite Thai food restaurant where he placed a large to-go order. Just because she didn't want to be intimate with him didn't mean they still couldn't enjoy a meal together.

Plus, he knew she wouldn't be able to resist the Pad Thai he smelled wafting from the kitchen.

Jonas slung the bags over his arms as he placed the key in the lock and pushed the door open. Inside, his condo was dim, as the sun was just setting. It was quiet. He checked his watch. It was just after six. Where was Mae? She would have definitely been home by now.

He walked to the kitchen and placed the bags on the counter.

"Mae?" he called out. There was no response.

He strolled down the hallway to her room and saw that her door was open. The sunset cast an orange hue through her room. He saw her lying on her bed sleeping. He smiled to himself. Last night must have worn her out. He felt it, too. Quietly, he walked toward the bed and admired her for a moment before gently pulling a blanket over her. He wished he could curl up beside her, but instead he quietly left the room, closing the door behind him.

Chapter 15

Mae

Mae stood in the bakery, drooling over the cakes on display in the glass case. They were simple, but elegantly decorated one-tier cakes and intricate three-tier wedding cakes. She admired each one, smiling to herself and taking in the sweet scents of the bakery.

"That white lace wedding cake is stunning." Wendy said, stepping beside her and pointing at the case.

Mae nodded. She had agreed to help Wendy choose some last-minute baked goods for the festival's dessert table, which was just a week away. This wasn't something she normally did. She was Braydon's assistant and mostly dealt with team-business only. But right now, the festival came first, and it was all hands on deck to see that it went off without a hitch. Besides, she was happy to be out of the office and away from Jonas after their night together.

"Have you thought much about your wedding?" Wendy asked.

Mae looked at her dumbfounded. Did Wendy know? She didn't know what to say.

"I just mean was it something you dreamed about as a little girl? All these wedding cakes make me think of my special day. It will be beautiful when your day comes," Wendy said wistfully.

Mae let out a little sigh of relief. She didn't know.

"I definitely thought about it when I was younger. The whole storybook romance and a big wedding. Seeing my parents so in love gave me something to look forward to."

"It must be hard without them."

"It is."

"Well, I'm sure they're looking down on you. They would want to see you happy."

Mae nodded. She didn't talk much about her parents with anyone besides Nico.

"So, are you seeing anyone?" Wendy asked.

Mae shook her head and pretended to study the display case.

"And why not? You're a successful, beautiful girl," said Wendy with a motherly tone.

"There's just not enough time, especially when you have Braydon as a boss."

"You forget who you're talking to. Jonas is my boss, remember?"

Mae laughed. "Touché."

"Still, you don't want to end up like him. All alone. You should get out there." Wendy touched Mae's arm gently.

Mae nodded. "I'll think about it."

She felt bad for lying to Wendy. She was always so nice to her and would honestly be thrilled to hear about the marriage to Jonas. She was almost like a second mother to him. Along with the rest of the office, she would know soon. But even then, Mae would still be lying because the relationship wasn't real.

When it was their turn in line, Wendy and Mae placed their order and headed back to the office, which was bustling. You'd think they were in the party planning business, rather than owning a baseball team. Dollies of decorations were being wheeled in, checklists were being crossed off, and confirmations were being made over the phone.

Mae spotted Jonas talking closely with a petite party planner. She had dark brown hair cut into a sleek bob and full lips, and was leaning a little too close to him. Jonas placed his hand on her back as they went through the papers on her clipboard. Mae felt a hint of jealousy creep in. Not that she had any right to be jealous. She had let Jonas know where they stood.

What happened the other night couldn't happen again. As good as it was—okay, as amazing as it was—it had been a mistake. In the moment, she had let herself enjoy it thoroughly, and especially enjoyed cuddling by the fireplace until they fell asleep wrapped around each other. She had watched Jonas doze off and told herself she would feel like a fool in the morning, and she did. Their night together had filled her heart, but broken it at the same time because none of it was real.

Just then, Jonas looked up at her and flashed that smile of his. Mae watched as he excused himself from the party planner and beelined toward her. She couldn't help but let out a little laugh at the party planner's face that had morphed into a frown, as she watched wistfully after her prospect.

"Mae. How are you?" asked Jonas as he stepped in front of her.

"Better than her." She nodded toward the party planner.

Jonas glanced over his shoulder quickly and shook his head. "Oh, her? That was nothing. Just finalizing the details for the auction."

"Doesn't matter. You're free to do what you want." Mae shrugged nonchalantly.

"Nope. I'm a married man," said Jonas, pointing at his ring. "I only have eyes for my wife."

Mae rolled her eyes, but internally, she felt her heart skip.

"Anyway. Wendy and I placed the order at the bakery. Everything will be delivered the day of the festival."

"Good, good. Thanks again for helping out. I want everything to go perfectly, especially for our big announcement."

"Mhmm." Mae looked down at her feet.

"Nico still not talking to you?"

"Nope."

Jonas put his hand on her shoulder and smiled reassuringly. "He will."

Braydon came up behind them and put his arms around them lovingly. "Look at you lovebirds."

"Braydon. Shhh," said Mae under her breath.

"All right, all right," said Braydon as he backed away with his hands up. "I have to say, I can't wait for the festival, so I don't have to tiptoe around anymore."

"Same here," said Jonas as he eyed Mae lovingly.

Mae looked up at him before quickly looking away. Gosh, he was really good at this whole pretend thing. She had to remind herself it was all for show.

"If you'll excuse me, I have to make a phone call." She pulled her cellphone from her purse and walked away. She needed to get away. How was she supposed to distance her feelings from Jonas when they were about to go public with their relationship? It was hard enough putting on a show for Braydon, but now they had to show the world how in love they were. She wasn't sure if she would be able to distinguish between the façade and reality.

She needed to talk to someone. She scrolled through her phone and stopped at her best friend, Lindsay, and hit the call button. After a few rings, she heard the other line pick up and her best friend yelling.

"Jack, get down from the table! You're going to give me a heart attack. Ellie, don't feed the dogs!"

There was the sound of clatter and dogs barking and then heavy breathing.

"Hello?" said Mae.

"Oh shoot. Hello? Who is this?"

"It's me."

"Mae! Hi! I'm so sorry. It's a madhouse over here."

"I hear that."

"These kids are trying to kill me," whispered Lindsay dramatically.

Mae let out a laugh. Lindsay had been her best friend since high school, and although their lives were drastically different, they still remained closer than ever. Lindsay lived in the suburbs, close to Mae's old house. She was married to her high school sweetheart, Brad, and they had two kids, Jack and Ellie.

"Who said having two under two was a good idea?" asked Lindsay, exasperated.

"Uh, you did. You said you wanted to get it all over with in one swoosh."

"Oh, right."

"How would you like to meet me in the city for lunch?" asked Mae enticingly.

"Now?"

"Mhmm."

"You're speaking my language. I'll be there in an hour."

When Mae walked through the front door of Mabel's, she saw Lindsay already at the bar being served a glass of wine.

"You starting without me?" asked Mae, taking the seat next to her.

"Oh, hi. I got here a little early. Brad has the day off, so I got out of there before he could change his mind."

Mae signaled the bartender. "I'll have what she's having."

After Mae was served, they clinked their wine glasses together and took a sip.

"Mmmm." Lindsay closed her eyes. "Just what mama needed."

"Same," said Mae, letting out a sigh.

Lindsay opened her eyes and shot Mae a look. "What's up?" she asked skeptically.

"Nothing." Mae shrugged innocently.

"I've known you for fourteen years. I know when something's up."

Mae took a sip of wine. As much as she wanted to talk to her friend, she all of a sudden felt nervous to tell her about the arrangement with Jonas. Lindsay knew how much he had hurt her. She hoped she wouldn't judge her too harshly.

As if reading her mind, Lindsay touched Mae's arm. "Whatever it is, you can tell me. I know you didn't drag me out of the suburbs for nothing."

Mae looked down at her lap before raising her left hand.

"Mae! What is that?" Lindsay grabbed her hand excitedly, examining the ring.

"Surprise," said Mae warily.

"It's huge! This probably costs more than my house! Wait, there's a wedding band…"

"I kinda got married."

"What?!" shouted Lindsay.

"Shhhh," said Mae, giving her a little shove.

"When?"

"A few weeks ago."

"*Excuse* me? And I'm just now finding out. And wait, why wasn't I invited?"

"We eloped."

Lindsay nodded as if trying to process all this new information. Mae sat with bated breath as she waited for the next question.

"Well, who is he?" Lindsay raised an eyebrow.

"You know him, actually."

"I do?"

"Mhmm." Mae nervously took a sip of wine as she watched Lindsay put the pieces into place.

"The only person I know who could afford that," said Lindsay slowly, eyeing the ring, "is an asshole who you said you would never give another chance to."

"I did say that…"

"Mae!" shouted Lindsay again.

168

"Let me explain!"

Mae told her the entire thing. How Jonas had approached her with this arrangement and how he threatened Nico's career. How she lives with him and how they're going to go public soon.

"He is diabolical." Lindsay shook her head.

"He's really not that bad," said Mae softly.

"He basically blackmailed you into marrying him. Fake marrying him. Whatever this is. And he's not *that* bad?"

"He seems different from before."

"Please, tell me you're not falling for him again?"

"No, but we did share a moment the other night."

"Tell me you did not have sex with him."

Mae shrugged sheepishly.

Lindsay shook her head. "You're smarter than this, Mae. He's going to break your heart again."

Mae didn't say anything because she knew her friend was right. She fought back tears as she stared at the ring on her finger.

"I'm sorry." Lindsay brought her in for a hug. "I just love you, and I don't want you to get hurt again."

"I know." Mae nodded.

They hugged for a moment longer.

169

"Please, come to the festival," said Mae, forcing a smile.

"No way." Lindsay shook her head.

"It will be fun. You can bring Brad and the kids. Plus, we need to see each other more."

Lindsay thought it over for a moment. Mae clasped her hands together and silently begged.

"Fine." Lindsay rolled her eyes. "But I'm not guaranteeing I won't punch him square in the face."

"You'll have to wait in line." Mae laughed.

"You better get us good tickets."

"VIP. Only the best for you." Mae gave her friend a big hug and squeezed her. "Thank you," she whispered.

"I'm always here for you," Lindsay replied as she squeezed her back.

On her walk back to the office, Mae smiled to herself. As tough of a conversation as that was, she felt like a weight was lifted off her shoulders. She didn't realize how much she needed to talk to someone, especially because Nico had been avoiding her since their argument. Their rift was something she would have to tackle at another time. For now, she was ready to focus on work and the festival. Her personal life would have to take the back-burner.

She could use the distraction, anyway. Now, if only the person she needed distracting from wasn't someone she worked with—and lived with.

Chapter 16

Jonas

Jonas took a sip of coffee as he walked beside Victoria. She checked off her to-do list maniacally. She was the best party planner in Boston and not too hard on the eyes, either. Maybe that was why she was a hot commodity. As Victoria rambled on, he smiled to himself thinking of Mae's expression earlier. He could have sworn he saw jealousy wash over her when she spotted him and Victoria working earlier.

Even though Mae had tried to act nonchalant about it, Jonas could see right through her. Despite where they left things after spending that night together, he got a glimpse of how Mae really felt. Or at least, how he hoped she felt. In the past, Jonas would have used a woman like Victoria to his benefit to rub it in Mae's face. But today, when he saw her watching them, the last thing he wanted to do was play games.

"It looks like we're missing an order of champagne," Victoria said, counting the stacked boxes in the conference room.

Stressed, Jonas rubbed his cheeks as he let out a sigh. Victoria placed her hand on his arm and gave a gentle squeeze. "I'll take care of it," she said reassuringly. She pulled out her phone and began typing out an email aggressively.

"You're scary," said Jonas jokingly.

"You have no idea."

"I guess that's why you're one of the best."

"I am the best, darling. And I always get what I want." Victoria's eyes narrowed in on Jonas's lips.

"Well, let's hope nothing else goes wrong," said Jonas, looking at the boxes and trying to avoid Victoria's seductive stare.

As much as everything had been planned and scheduled for months now, Jonas knew that nothing ever went one hundred percent smoothly. He hoped this missing box of champagne was the worst of his problems. This was his first time in charge of the annual festival since his dad passed, and there was so much to prove. People came from all over Boston to support the team and its charity.

"How is everything going with the auction?" asked Jonas.

"Everything is all set. Every vendor has sent in product for the raffle."

"And for the auction?"

"The auction jerseys for the players are being pressed and will be delivered to each player. That will be the money maker. Every cougar in Boston will be paying big bucks for a date with a major league player."

"That was the idea," said Jonas proudly. He had thought of it himself.

"How much do you think *I* would go for?" asked Victoria, leaning her back against the wall. Jonas couldn't help looking at her breasts, which she pushed out proudly as she played with her necklace.

"I doubt there is a number high enough." Jonas leaned casually against the wall. It felt good to be wanted, but he knew he was on dangerous ground.

"For you, I'd let you take me out for free." Victoria bit her lip as she slid her hand across the wall and shut the conference door, locking it.

Victoria walked toward him. Jonas felt tense but didn't move. Normally, he would welcome a beautiful woman coming on to him, but now he just felt nervous. Guilty. He felt her hands travel up his chest and around his neck as she pressed her body against his. She looked up at him through her long lashes with a lustful smile.

"Do you know how hard it's been working so close to you, and not being able to do the one thing running through my head?" she whispered in his ear.

"And what's that?"

"I think you know." She slid her hands to his groin.

Just then, he felt his phone vibrate in his jacket pocket. It seemed to break him out of whatever spell he was under. He didn't even know what he was doing. He couldn't do this to Mae. Jonas took Victoria's hand, moved it away, and slipped his phone out of his pocket.

"Is that important?" asked Victoria, annoyed.

"Afraid so," said Jonas, sliding away from her. "Hello?" he answered.

"Mr. Matthews?" a voice asked nervously on the other line.

"Yes?"

"This is Delvin's Catering. I'm so sorry to inform you we are no longer able to work the event on Friday."

"You're kidding?" Jonas asked, exasperated.

"I wish I was. Our water heater flooded our kitchen, and it's inoperable. We were so looking forward to working the event, as we have been a partner for years. I can put you in touch with other vendors…"

"No. I don't want another vendor. People are expecting Delvin's on the table. I'm coming down there."

"But—"

Jonas hung up and plopped down in a chair.

Victoria glared at him. "Bad news?"

"Yes, Delvin's backed out. But you have enough on your plate."

"I'm willing to help. Whatever you need." She sat in the chair next to him, trailing her finger up his arm. This woman was relentless.

Jonas looked down at her hand. Clearly, she was not getting the hint.

"That's quite all right," he said as he crossed his arms. "My *wife* is great at this stuff."

Victoria recoiled as if she had just been bit on the hand by a snake. She nodded and stood up slowly.

"Well, I better get back to my to-do list," she said curtly.

"Yes, that's probably best. Thank you."

Jonas stood swiftly and walked out of the conference room. He felt like an idiot. He was so close to making a mistake. Mae didn't deserve that, fake married or not. As he made his way

176

back to his office, he scrolled through his contacts until he landed on Mae's number. He wasn't about to tell her what happened with Victoria, not after he reassured her he only wanted her. It was the truth, but sometimes old habits died hard.

He could really use Mae's help with this vendor mishap, and truthfully, he just wanted to see her. To be close to her. He knew she could calm him down, and right now he was stressed.

Delvin's was a city favorite. It was a popular place on game day because of the sports paraphernalia all over the walls. They served the best gourmet game day food. The owner had been close with Jonas's father. They *had* to be a part of the festival. It was tradition.

He typed out *SOS* and hit send. He watched impatiently. Finally, three dots appeared and he waited for her to respond.

Mae: *In a meeting with Braydon. Be there soon.*

Jonas smiled and set his phone on his desk.

Fifteen minutes later, he heard a soft knock at his door.

"Yes?"

"It's me." Mae pushed open the door and waited at the door hesitantly.

Jonas smiled and waved her in. "Come in, come in. That was a quick meeting," he said, checking his watch.

"Braydon said it was a wife's duty to help her husband when he's in need." Mae rolled her eyes and took a seat across from him. "So, what's up? Why the SOS?"

"Delvin's just called to back out."

"What? Oh, my gosh. They're our biggest vendor."

"I know. This is bad, Mae. I can just feel my father laughing at my failures."

Mae looked at him with a surprised sadness in her eyes. He hardly ever opened up about his father, especially since his passing. The pressure was mounting more than ever, though. He just needed someone to talk to. Not someone. Mae.

"Jonas." She reached over and put her hand over his. It was soft and smooth, and sent warmth through his fingers and arm. He looked at her hand on his. *This* was what he needed.

"Look at me," said Mae gently.

Jonas looked up and met her gaze.

"Despite the relationship with your father, I think he would be proud of you. He left this job to you because he knew you could do it."

"I'm not so sure lately."

178

"Well, I'm sure," she said, giving his hand a squeeze.

"This is my big chance to prove myself. To have people see that I am capable."

"Jonas, you're the hardest worker I know. Everyone knows it. Hell, you broke my heart because of it."

"Mae—" Jonas looked at her remorsefully.

She waved him away. "The past is in the past. I'm just saying, people are well aware of what you're capable of. We will sort out a new food vendor. Everything is going to be okay."

He watched as she smiled at him, nodding reassuringly. She really believed in him. He was so thankful for her in that moment. Maybe she was what he needed. Why couldn't there be work and love, especially if it was with someone who supported you?

"Thank you, Mae," he said softly.

"Of course. Now, how can I help, *hubby*?" she asked with a grin

"I need you to try and find a new vendor. I'll send Wendy with you, as she has a list of contacts."

Mae nodded. "It's last minute, but we will try. What are *you* going to do?"

"I'm going to head over there to Delvin's to yell at them."

"That sounds like a *great* idea," she said sarcastically.

"I need to blow off a little steam."

"There are other ways to do that," she said, raising her eyebrows.

He narrowed his eyes at her. "I know, but you made it clear that we could never do *that* again."

He watched Mae blush as he buzzed Wendy on his desk phone. "Wendy, can you come in here, please."

A few moments later, Wendy entered the office. Jonas filled her in on their dilemma.

"I'll head out and start looking for vendors right away," Wendy assured him.

"I'm sending Mae with you. You two did a great job at the bakery this morning."

"We make a good team," said Mae.

"Of course you do. My two best ladies," said Jonas as he stood from his desk. He walked around and leaned down to kiss Mae. Her eyes widened with surprise, but she closed them as soon as their lips met. When he pulled away, Mae looked up at him with a curious smile. Wendy's mouth hung wide open as she looked between the two of them slowly.

180

"Well, we should be going," said Mae with a laugh of disbelief. She grabbed Wendy's hand and pulled her out of the office. Jonas smiled after her.

It wasn't until he was on his way to Delvin's that he realized what he had done.

"Well, fuck," said Jonas as he sat in the town car, buildings whirring by.

Kissing Mae had come so naturally, like she was really his wife. Maybe it was that moment with Victoria that put things into perspective. Maybe it was knowing he could count on Mae. Maybe it was because she was so beautiful. Or that she believed in him. He hadn't kissed her for show, or to prove anything was real. Wendy didn't even know about them. But she did now. No wonder she looked so caught off guard. They gave her a shock, that was for sure.

This whole charade wasn't supposed to feel so natural. It wasn't supposed to be real. He made that pact with himself from the get-go. Obviously, choosing Mae for this arrangement would blur things a little, but he never intended to let real feelings emerge. If sex were a part of it, he wouldn't complain. In the end, this was supposed to be strictly business. As much as he tried to deny it, he knew this was no longer a business arrangement.

Jonas let out a frustrated sigh. If his father wasn't laughing before, Jonas was positive he was now. He shook his head. This could only end badly. He couldn't dwell on it now though. He had just pulled up in front of Delvin's. He needed his head on straight to sort this out, even though his head was filled with Mae.

Chapter 17

Mae

Wendy and Mae pulled up to Richie's Gourmet Hotdogs and parked. The restaurant was bustling, which was a good sign that it was well liked in the city. They hoped Richie's could lock them down for the festival that was just days away. Although they had never worked together in the past, it would be good exposure for the restaurant.

Mae went to open her car door, but Wendy stayed put in the passenger seat.

"Aren't we heading in?" asked Mae, her hand still on the door handle.

"You're just going to act like nothing just happened?" asked Wendy, playfully raising her eyebrow.

"What?" Mae shrugged innocently.

Wendy shook her head with a smile. "Fine. Be like that. But I'll get it out of one of you. Eventually."

Mae avoided Wendy's gaze and eyed the restaurant. "We should go in and beat the lunchtime rush."

The two women walked inside and were hit with the smell of caramelized onions and broiled bacon. There were only a few empty booths, and the patrons were chattily eating. Mae watched as a hot dog wrapped in a fresh croissant, next to a hot dog loaded with melted cheese and jalapenos, passed by on a tray. The walls were filled with photos of celebrities who had dined there, along with sports paraphernalia.

"This place looks well loved." Mae nudged Wendy and nodded at a picture of the president holding a hot dog.

"I think I saw this place on the *Food Network*."

"Can I get you ladies a table?" The hostess smiled as she stacked menus.

"Actually, is there a manager we can talk to? We would like to discuss a potential business opportunity," said Wendy.

"I'll do you one better. The owner is back in the kitchen. I'll be right back."

A few moments later, a short, round man emerged from the kitchen and flashed them a smile. He held out his hand and Mae shook it firmly, followed by Wendy.

"I'm Rick, but you can call me Richie. I own the place. Chrissy says you're here on business.

What can I help you ladies with?" he asked curiously.

"We are with the Matthews Group. We are in a bit of a pinch and hoping you could help us out."

"Matthews Group? As in our team's owner?" He nodded toward a large photo of the city's original team.

"That's right." Mae nodded.

"I'm all ears."

Mae explained their predicament with the festival and the need for a vendor. Thankfully, Richie was eager to be a vendor, but not for a small fee. Wendy negotiated him down, but it was still beyond budget. With the festival approaching rapidly, they had no other choice. Plus, they needed a vendor that would impress their guests and Richie's was clearly well loved.

As they drove back to the office, Wendy began drawing up a contract on her phone to get sent to Richie within the hour. Mae was thankful she had something to keep her busy so she wouldn't ask any more questions.

Back in her own office, Mae shut the door and plopped down in her desk chair. She breathed a sigh of relief, not only for the new vendor, but to be away from Wendy. She thought back to the kiss. Jonas had looked so comfortable as he leaned down to kiss her. He looked so happy. It was like they were the only two in the room. It seemed so genuine. Mae smiled to herself as she remembered the look on Wendy's face. She thought her jaw actually hit the floor. Mae laughed to herself, but then the doubt began to creep in.

Had he kissed her just for show? But why would he do it in front of Wendy, who had no idea? Braydon, it would be understandable. Wendy had no idea about them, though. So far, Jonas had been a pretty good actor. She'd tried her best to match him and play along. Maybe he was just preparing himself for when they went public at the festival. Then everyone would know.

Mae didn't really think about it until now. She'd been so busy with work that she never realized that once everyone knew, kisses in public would be frequent. She wasn't sure if she would be able to handle the intimacy without letting her feelings complicate things. Already, Mae had already let them get the best of her when she basically threw herself at Jonas.

Then, there was Nico to worry about. He still wasn't talking to her, and his absence from her life was starting to dwell on her. They had never gone this long without talking. She hoped her parents weren't looking down on them with sadness. Just thinking about it, she could cry. She put her face in her hands and tried to hold back tears.

A knock sounded at her door, breaking her from her thoughts, which she was thankful for. She cleared her throat and tried to compose herself.

"Come in," she called.

Braydon entered her office. "I heard you landed Richie's!" he said with an impressed nod.

"We did. I think it will be a welcome addition to the festival. Maybe it can turn into a long-term partnership."

"We're really changing things up this year with auctioning off the players accompanied by new food."

"You think it's too much?"

"No, I think it's what the festival needs. It's been the same thing year after year. While tradition is great, it's good to keep people on their toes."

Mae nodded.

"Plus, your husband needs to establish himself outside his father's shadow."

"Good point. I think he's doing a good job so far."

"You two make a good team." Braydon winked.

"Yeah, we do."

"Which is why I think you should work more closely with him. At least until the festival is over."

"What? Won't you need me?" asked Mae with surprise.

"Nah. I've been in this business longer than you've been born, my dear. Plus, I'm heading off to scout the day after the festival. You should stay back to celebrate."

"Celebrate what?"

"Hmm, let's see. A successful festival. An engagement *and* a marriage."

"I've been busy." Mae smiled.

"Too busy. I want you to soak it in a bit."

"Thank you, Braydon." She stood from her desk and walked over to him. He gave her a big bear hug. Even though he was her boss, he had become a father figure to her over the years. As much as he relied on her, maybe too much at times, he always had her well-being in mind.

"Now, before I lend you to Jonas, I do need you to go through the list of games and come up with a schedule for me," Braydon said, pulling out his phone.

Mae nodded as she sat down and opened up her laptop. For the next two hours, they went through all the games in the country and came up with an itinerary. It was a lot of work going through flights and hotels, but she was happy for it. It kept her mind off of Jonas and how complicated everything was about to get.

When she left the office that evening, she decided to walk back to Jonas's. She was in no rush to be near him, not with feelings around every corner. She window-shopped along the way and popped into her favorite corner market to peruse the wine. She chose a nice bottle of Merlot and finally walked the block home. Jonas's home.

When she walked into the condo, Jonas was on the couch scrolling on his phone. He wore a baggy team sweatshirt and black sweats. He looked good in anything and it frustrated her. It also frustrated her that he had been home every day by 5:30. He had taken his self-challenge seriously, and she regretted making it an issue.

"You've proven your point," she said pointedly.

He looked up from his phone and raised an eyebrow questioningly.

"You don't live and breathe work. I get it." She waved her finger in the air in a small, sarcastic celebration.

Jonas let out a laugh. "What, you're sick of me already? It hasn't even been a full week."

"I'm just saying, with the festival, I would understand you staying late." She shrugged.

"It almost sounds like you're trying to get rid of me."

Mae didn't respond and headed to the kitchen to set her market bag down. She felt Jonas following behind her. She let out a breath and ignored him as he sidled up next to her. She inhaled his bodywash. It matched his cologne, which had lingered on her body since that night together.

"What did you get at the market?" he asked, taking a peek inside the bag.

"Just some wine and a few little groceries." She began to unpack.

He started to help her put things away, but she stopped him. "You don't have to do that." She shook her head.

He stopped short in the middle of the kitchen, holding a carton of bruschetta. He gave her a curious look as he placed it back on the counter.

"Is this about Braydon?" he asked.

"What? That he's *lending* me to you?"

"Is that a bad thing?"

"Did you put the idea in his head?" she asked, sharper than she intended.

"No…" said Jonas hesitantly. "He came up with it all on his own. Although, I could use the help. You really saved my ass today with Richie's."

Mae nodded and continued putting the groceries away. After, she walked to the bar with her bottle of wine and pulled down a stemless glass from the shelf. She poured herself a generous serving and took a sip, closing her eyes. With her eyes still closed, she felt Jonas come up behind her. She wanted nothing more than to lean back and feel the warmth of his body, but she also wanted nothing more than to distance herself. She was torn.

"Mae," he whispered.

"Hmm?" She didn't turn around.

"Did I do something wrong?" he asked softly.

Why was he being so nice? It frustrated her. She turned around to face him.

"Why do you do that?" she asked sharply.

"What?" He shrugged.

"Why are you being so… so…" She felt exasperated.

"So *what?*" he asked innocently.

191

"So nice? Why are you acting like you're *actually* my husband?"

"Well, we have to be convincing…"

"We aren't in front of anyone now. And that kiss in front of Wendy? She didn't even know about us."

Jonas stayed silent as he looked at his hands. She wanted him to admit that he was struggling with the same feelings as she was. She wanted him to tell her that he wanted her. For real. She waited for a moment for him to look at her. To say something. But he just stood there.

Mae grabbed her glass of wine, causing it to slosh onto the counter. She didn't care. She walked swiftly to her bathroom and shut the door behind her, locking it. She couldn't be around Jonas right now. She was too angry, and the last time she was angry she ended up falling asleep on his chest.

Taking a deep breath, Mae set her wine glass on the counter and looked at herself in the mirror. She shook her head at herself. How could she have been so stupid? This whole arrangement had been a bad idea from the start, but she did it for Nico. Who wasn't even speaking to her. A small part of her wondered if she had agreed for other reasons.

She pushed herself from the counter and drew a hot bath, pouring a generous amount of bubble bath in. Once the bubbles were almost overflowing, she turned the water off and undressed. As the hot water washed over her, she leaned her head back and looked up at the ceiling. She would hide out here all night if it meant she wouldn't have any more encounters with Jonas.

Chapter 18

Jonas

Jonas rolled over in bed and hit his alarm clock. Then he rolled back over onto his stomach and groaned into the pillow. He hadn't slept well. He had tossed and turned most of the night, thinking about the festival, which was tomorrow, and thinking about Mae, who had managed to avoid him all last night. Not an easy feat when you lived together.

She hadn't even come out of her room for dinner. Jonas had ordered sushi for takeout and had eaten by himself. When he had knocked on her bedroom door to offer dinner, she had said she wasn't hungry. This was unusual for Mae who loved food, which was what he loved about her. She had an appetite. He did hear her rummaging around in the kitchen around midnight. Clearly, her hunger strike had run out.

He rolled out of bed and headed to the bathroom to take a cold shower. He hoped it would wake him up. It was a big day full of final details. He had pawned that party planner Victoria off onto Wendy, so he wouldn't have to deal with her. Mae was supposed to be his assistant for the day, but after last night, he wasn't confident in their teamwork.

After his shower, which was more uncomfortable than waking, he headed to the kitchen to make a big carafe of coffee. He was surprised to see Mae already in the kitchen making breakfast. She was not an early riser. She stood with her back to him, cooking eggs on the stovetop in one of Jonas's team sweatshirts. He leaned against the wall and admired her.

"My sweatshirt looks good on you," he said.

Mae whirled around and looked at him, nearly dropping the salt and pepper.

"You scared me," she said with an annoyed look on her face. "And what do you mean *your* sweatshirt? This is mine." She looked down at the red fleece and pulled at it.

"There's a hole in the back from when it snagged on a post at one of the games."

Mae looked over her shoulder and saw the hole he was talking about, which gave a glimpse of her lace panties. She gasped and covered her behind immediately. Jonas let out a laugh.

"No wonder it felt big. I have the same one." She blushed. "I'll give it back."

"Hand it over." Jonas held out his hand.

"Oh, shut up." She held back a smile.

She continued cooking the eggs at an awkward angle, with her back to the counter. Jonas shook his head and made his way to the coffeemaker. He worked the settings for two large cups of coffee and the smell of French roast filled the kitchen. He sat at the kitchen counter and scrolled through the news on his phone. Mae pushed a plate of eggs and bacon in front of him.

"Thank you. This looks great," said Jonas gratefully.

She nodded and scooted to the other side of the kitchen to eat in silence. Clearly, she still didn't want to be near him. Jonas didn't want to press her on it because they had a long day ahead of working together. There was no need to rock the boat. They could talk about whatever was going on with her another time. Jonas finished his breakfast and placed his plate in the dishwasher, leaving Mae in the kitchen alone. He could have sworn he heard her let out a sigh of relief as he walked away.

After Jonas shaved and dressed for work, he found the house empty. His red sweatshirt lay on the arm of the couch. Mae's purse was gone from the entryway table. She must have left early for work. Again, another sign that something was up with her. While she was never late for work, she wasn't exactly eager to get there, either. Jonas huffed. What was up with her? He was trying not to let it nag at him. She couldn't honestly avoid him all day. They had work to do.

When he arrived in his office, he noticed Wendy was away from her desk. *She must be with Victoria,* he thought. He began going through his emails and making phone calls. His fingers thumped on his desk while he sat, wondering where Mae was. He'd been at the office for two hours already. They had an afternoon meeting to plan. Maybe she had forgotten that she was his assistant for the remainder of the week. He began writing his ideas on post-its and sticking them up and down his desk.

"There has to be a better method for that." Mae leaned against the doorframe, eyeing the colored paper.

"Mae, there you are," said Jonas, standing up nervously. Why did he stand up? He stood awkwardly for a moment and then sat back down. He watched Mae hold back a smile as she took a seat in front of him.

"I got caught up with a schedule conflict for Braydon's trip."

"Oh. That's all right. I was beginning to think you were avoiding me."

"Maybe a little," she said softly.

He furrowed his brow. "Why?"

"I've just been going through a lot, and you tend to complicate things."

"Who, me?" Jonas asked, acting innocent, holding his hand to his chest.

"Oh, stop. Now, let me look at these post-its."

For the next hour they went through the talking points for the meeting. It was close to feeling normal. Mae was closer than she had been the past two days, but that was only because she *had* to be. Still, Jonas was happy for it. He breathed in her perfume and studied her face as she concentrated on working through his idea of organization. He loved the way her brow furrowed when she was studying his handwriting. He loved when one blonde tendril of hair would fall in her face and she would tuck it behind her ear, only for it to fall thirty seconds later. He loved the way she placed the tip of her pen against her lips, which sat like plush, pink pillows on her perfect face.

She looked up and caught him staring intently. "What?" she asked, tilting her head.

"Nothing," he said softly, shaking his head.

She looked at him for a moment longer before accepting his answer.

"You should really get a notebook," she said, stacking the sticky notes on top of one another. "This is not the most efficient thing."

"It's worked for me," said Jonas, leaning back in his chair and looking around his office.

Mae rolled her eyes. "You ready for the meeting?" she asked.

"Are *you?* Nico is going to be there."

Jonas knew Mae's relationship with her brother had been rocky since he found out about them. At first, it was satisfying knowing how worked up Nico was. Of course, it was unprofessional to barge into his office like that, but clearly Jonas had finally gotten to him. Another bonus was the anger Mae felt that had led to some pretty amazing sex. But still, Jonas could see how the issue with her brother was wearing on Mae.

"I'll be fine. Just please don't try to rock the boat." She gave him a look.

"I'm not the one who came in here, guns blazing."

"I know. But still. Please, Jonas," she pled.

Jonas nodded. "Okay."

They stood up and walked down the hallway toward the elevator. They waited in silence until the doors opened. Jonas was surprised to see Wendy and Victoria standing inside. *This won't be awkward,* he thought sarcastically, as they stepped inside. He greeted them both with a tight smile, and pressed the button for the doors to close. He could feel Victoria's eyes burning a hole in him until she went on to looking Mae up and down judgmentally. Jonas stood a little closer to Mae, just to make his point. Wendy was smiling at them like a child. Yep, definitely awkward.

Jonas was relieved when they reached the conference room floor. Most of the office was sitting around the table, ready for the meeting. Jonas took a seat at the head of the table and Mae took the seat next to him. Just then, the team ambled through the door loudly.

"Quiet down, boys," said their new trainer, who was trailing behind them.

The team nodded in unison and leaned against the back wall. They weren't usually at meetings, but since they were a big part of tomorrow's festival, they had been called in. Jonas spotted Nico, who was staring down at his feet, making it clear he had no interest in being there. He looked to Mae, who glanced at her brother sadly before going through the stack of sticky notes. He needed to make this right. Eventually.

"Thank you all for being here," said Jonas as he stood up. "I appreciate all the hard work everyone has put in this week to make sure our festival is a success. There are a few final details to discuss for the day of."

He turned to Mae, who began listing off different tasks. Everyone listened intently while typing notes into their phones and adding to-dos to their planners.

"Now, about the auction. I hope you boys are ready," said Jonas, looking at the team.

"Bring on the cougars!" shouted Chad as he beat his chest.

The team whooped and slapped each other on the back.

"All right, all right. Calm down," said Jonas, biting back a smile. He was happy they were so enthusiastic about being auctioned off.

"Obviously, all dates will be at a select location with security," he continued. "Your safety is important to us."

"Hey now. I wouldn't mind someone getting handsy with me." Chad winked as the team laughed and nodded in agreement.

"Obviously, this is in good fun. The chance to 'buy' a player for the night is going to raise a lot of money for charity. I appreciate you all being such good sports," said Jonas.

"How much do you think I'm worth, ladies?" Chad lifted his jersey to show off his six-pack abs to the ladies in the office. Most of them rolled their eyes and laughed. Wendy fanned herself.

"I'm more interested to see if Nico's sister is up for auction," someone called out.

Jonas was taken aback. He looked up suddenly to see Marco, the team's trainer, smiling at Mae suggestively.

"She's not," said Nico pointedly.

"Aw, come on, man. Just for the night. Rumor is, she likes office relationships."

Jonas watched the color drain from Mae's face as she swallowed hard and looked down at her hands, which were visibly shaking. Jonas felt heat rush up his neck to his cheeks as he squeezed his fists together. It took everything in him to keep his cool. The whole office was watching the exchange with their mouths open.

"Like Nico said, she's not up for auction," he said coolly.

Marco held up his hands innocently. "It was just a question."

"And that question just got you fired."

"Hey, man, don't be like that. It was just a joke."

"Get out." Jonas narrowed his eyes.

Marco stood there staring at Jonas in shock, but didn't budge.

"I'll give you a hand with the trash, boss." Nico grabbed Marco roughly by the arm, and his best friend, Kenny grabbed his other arm. They both pulled Marco outside of the conference room. The rest of the team followed. Jonas knew they all loved Mae and had her back.

Jonas watched as they left the room and turned back to the boring eyes of the office staff, which were all on him. Everyone waited with bated breath for what was coming next. This was probably the most dramatic meeting they've had.

"That will be all. Everyone out," said Jonas.

But no one moved.

Frustrated, Jonas said, "Did you not hear me? Show's over. Get back to work."

Wendy began shooing everyone toward the door. As everyone was silently gathering their things, he glanced at Mae, who was already looking up at him. Her head was tilted slightly, and her expression was unreadable.

Chapter 19

Mae

Mae sat in the conference room alone. She had stayed behind after everyone had cleared out. Jonas had hesitantly left her at the table, but only after she had assured him she was okay. She just needed a moment to process everything that had just happened.

When Marco initially asked his lewd question, she was prepared to roll her eyes and move on. She hadn't expected him to go on to air out dirty laundry. Where had he heard about her being in an office relationship? The rumors were starting to spread like wildfire and she didn't know how. She felt relief that everything would be revealed tomorrow. She almost wished she could announce her marriage to Jonas right then, to spite him and everyone else who may be judging her. But she didn't want to spoil the announcement. She wanted it to be special for some reason.

The only thing that had kept her from either punching him square in the jaw or bursting into tears was the fact that Nico took up for her. And

Jonas. Jonas, who so easily came to her defense and fired the jerk on the spot. It was impressive. It was also hot. Very hot.

That was why Mae had to take a few moments to herself to process her feelings of embarrassment turning to anger, to pride, and then to being turned on. Mae took a deep breath and finally gathered her things, leaving the conference room. She didn't know what she was about to do, but she knew she had to see Jonas. She pressed the *down* button for the elevator and rode down, hoping she could sort out her next move in the ten seconds it took to reach his floor. She walked swiftly past Wendy's desk and opened Jonas's door, not bothering to knock.

He looked up at her, surprised by her barging in. She closed the door behind her and pressed her back against it. She studied Jonas for a moment. He sat at his desk in the charcoal gray suit she loved. His hair was pushed back, except for the unruly piece that always made its way into his eyes. His dark blue eyes wandered over her, eventually landing on hers. She let herself fall into them for a moment before something took over her.

Mae took a few confident strides to his desk. She knew what she wanted. As much as she hated

Jonas sometimes, she wanted him even more. He looked up at her curiously as she placed her hands on his desk and leaned forward, pushing her breasts together. She watched as his eyes wandered down to where her breasts peeked out from her silk camisole. He slowly looked up at her. She bit her bottom lip as she leaned in closer. Her face was just inches away and she could feel his breath against her mouth.

His eyes met hers. "I thought you didn't want—"

Mae put a finger to his lips. "Don't talk."

She grabbed the collar of his shirt and pulled him in, pressing her lips against his. His lips were soft. She parted hers slightly, allowing his tongue to slowly slide in and meet hers. She breathed him in. This was all she had wanted. Why had she fought this so much when it was all she thought about?

She felt her desire blooming as their mouths moved in a slow rhythm. The desk that separated them was an obstructive tease. She needed him closer. Taking his bottom lip in her teeth, she sucked gently before pulling away. Jonas groaned with pleasure as his eyes fluttered open, a fire starting in them.

Mae walked around the desk and he turned his chair to face her, leaning back expectantly. She liked that he was letting her take the lead. She reached for the zipper of her cream skirt and slowly unzipped it, letting it fall slowly and pool at her feet. His eyes wandered slowly down, as if lapping her up. She could see him fighting to keep still, and she smiled to herself. This power she had over him was giving her a thrill that heightened the sensation between her legs.

She leaned over Jonas and slowly lowered herself to sit facing him with her legs on either side. She looked at him intently as she pressed herself against his body. Jonas was growing hard through his pants, which made her suck in a breath. His eyes didn't leave hers as she began rubbing herself against him, grinding slowly. Even with the fabric between them, his erection caused her to tense as she felt electricity running through her.

His hands gripped her hips as she moved rhythmically. He grazed his lips against her neck, breathing against her as he kissed her just beneath her ear. He took her earlobe in his mouth and sucked gently. She let out a soft moan.

Suddenly, his hands were at her waist and he lifted her onto the edge of his desk. She let out a little gasp as he towered over her. Jonas placed his large hands on her thighs and pushed them apart easily. His eyes traveled down to her lace panties, which were already wet. He positioned himself between her legs, propping them open as his hands traveled up her thighs. Mae let her head fall backward as he stopped just shy of where she ached for him to touch her. He leaned down and ran his tongue against her lips as his fingers lightly traced against her. As he gently pulled the lace, revealing her to him, she shivered. Mae opened her mouth and took him in, just as his finger dipped inside her slowly, then gasped as he explored.

He pulled slowly out of her before easing two fingers inside. He moved slowly, massaging his palm against her. Their mouths stayed connected as they breathed each other in. Every shudder he felt pass through her pleased him. He pulled away and smiled at her, knowing that he was now in control. It was the sexiest look Mae had ever seen. She widened her legs and moved against his hand, enjoying every delicious second.

"Jonas," she moaned quietly into his ear. "I need you."

Her hands traveled, meeting his erection. She massaged her hand up and down through the fabric of his pants. Jonas groaned with pleasure, keeping his fingers inside her. Slowly, Mae unzipped his pants and his erection spilled out. She felt a rush through her whole body as she saw how hard he was. Closing her hand around him, she moved slowly down to his base. She felt him pause inside her as he let himself enjoy her massaging him. She moved up and down his shaft, watching the pleasure wash over his face.

With her other hand, she gently pulled his fingers from her wet tunnel and slowly slid off of him. He watched hungrily as she lowered to her knees, breathing against him. He closed his eyes as her tongue swirled against his tip. He tasted so good. She opened her mouth and took his tip in, sucking gently before moving her lips further down him.

"Mae," he moaned as his hands gripped the arms of the chair, his knuckles turning white.

She took him in fully, his erection reaching the back of her throat. Her mouth was warm and wet against him, as he filled her. She moved her mouth up and down, feeling him throb against her. Her hand met the base of him and moved in sync with her mouth. He was breathing heavily. Jonas grabbed her hair, his fingers tangled in her waves.

"Mae," he said it again, but more firmly this time. She slowly trailed her tongue up him as she pulled her lips away. When she looked up at him, he grabbed her face in his hands, pulling her to stand.

Jonas eased his pants down to his ankles, kicking them aside. In a second, he was between her legs, his erection inches away from her.

She locked eyes with him as she licked the palm of her hand before reaching down and gliding it down his shaft. She firmly gripped him as she shifted closer to the edge of the desk, opening her legs wide. He looked at her, wanting her. He thrusted slowly toward her, but she held him back with her hand. Mae looked up, running her tongue over her teasing smile.

He shook his head at her, a smile creeping over his lips. She eased him closer, allowing his tip to brush against her. She massaged her clit against him, watching his eyes watch them dance against each other, then pushed him away again before guiding him partly inside her. Mae held him in place as she moved herself up and down his tip. The control she had made her want to explode, but this build-up was too good to let go of yet.

Leaning back, Mae spread her legs wider as she guided him in further, but his rigid erection didn't fill her yet. She moved with ease onto him, her insides wet and enclosing him tightly. She clenched as she looked up at him. He tore his eyes away from down below and locked eyes with her. A look passed over him that made her shiver. She was in trouble now. The best kind. He shoved her hand aside and gripped her hips roughly, his fingertips pressing into her flesh.

"That's enough of that," he said firmly.

She let out a small raspy laugh before looking at him pleadingly.

He positioned himself in front of her before shoving every inch of him inside of her. It was so unexpected that it made her cry out in ecstasy. He pulled out just as quickly as he had entered, and met her again, slowly filling her this time. His hands still gripped her hips as he moved slowly in and out of her. Mae pulled her camisole over her head and let her breasts fall, much to his pleasure. His hands greedily moved to them, cupping them as he began to pump into her faster. He pushed her back, laying her back against the desk. Her breasts bounced with each thrust.

When she felt close to the edge, she sat up. She wasn't ready just yet. She pushed against his chest, causing him to stumble backward. With her eyes, she motioned for him to sit in his chair. He did as he was told and she was already climbing on top of him. She leaned over Jonas as he took her breasts in his mouth. Then she hovered over him before lowering herself. He groaned as he watched her slide onto him, taking him in entirely.

Mae positioned herself just right and began grinding against him. Slow at first, and then picking up the pace. She moved fluidly, gripping the back of his chair as he admired her body. She felt herself losing control and clenched tightly, unable to move. Seeing that she was at the edge, Jonas grabbed her from behind and moved her against him. His breathing became heavy and she could feel him throb inside her. She threw her head back and let out a loud moan as she exploded around him, and he let go inside her.

They remained wrapped around each other until their breathing slowed.

"Wow," whispered Jonas as he ran his fingers up and down her back.

"You can say that again," whispered Mae.

The way he held her, kissing her collarbone and looking at her with a softness she hadn't seen before, made Mae think that maybe this wouldn't end badly. Maybe it wouldn't end at all. And with that, she kissed him softly before laying her head on his shoulder.

Chapter 20

Jonas

The smell of kettle corn, hot dogs, and amber beer filled the stadium. Jonas breathed it all in as he took in the field. It was filled with people chattering and taking in the enormity of the city's beloved stadium. He loved seeing everything through their eyes. It was rare that the public had insider access or could be this close to the players. It only happened once a year, at this very festival.

Jonas remembered coming here as a child, alongside his father who had started the charity event a few years in as owner. The festival days were some of his fondest memories of his childhood. His father would take him from game to game, and let him eat all the cotton candy he wanted. Looking back, his father was probably just putting on a show, but back then Jonas had no idea. He had fun with his father and that was all that mattered.

When Jonas became owner, he knew he wanted to keep the tradition alive. It was the largest fundraiser they had all year, and all the proceeds went to the public schools. He was proud of it. Each year, it became bigger and better than before.

He smiled to himself as he walked amongst the games and vendors.

"This looks amazing, Jonas," said Mae, grabbing his hand and giving it a quick squeeze before pulling it away.

He looked at her and pulled her in close. She squirmed a little as she looked around nervously, until she settled into his embrace.

"What if people see?" she asked.

"So what? Let them. Everyone seems to know, anyway."

It was true. They hadn't even made their announcement yet, but the whole office seemed to know about them. Whoever had told Nico had spread it to everyone else. It was an unspoken thing, and people seemed to be happy for them.

Mae nodded, not quite convinced.

Jonas reached his hand up to her face and stroked her cheek. She looked up at him and gave him a soft smile. She really was beautiful, and he was so happy to share this special day with her. He knelt down and kissed her lips softly before pulling away to hear the sounds of Braydon cheering from the sidelines.

Mae rolled her eyes at him. "Are you happy now?" she called out.

"Very!" Braydon shouted before strolling away, whistling to himself.

"He is something else," said Jonas, shaking his head.

"I literally thought he was going to burst at the seams if he held onto that secret any longer." Mae giggled.

"Well, I don't know about you, but I'm happy to have it out in the open."

Mae nodded as they continued to walk the field.

Jonas bent down and whispered, "Although, it was kind of fun sneaking around."

She gave him a playful shove, but he knew she enjoyed it too. Their afternoon in his office yesterday was the best sex of his life. She had trembled on top of him as they ended in a tangled heap on his desk chair. He wondered if Wendy had heard. There was no way she hadn't. She did look a little flushed when he walked Mae out. He laughed to himself.

"What?" asked Mae, raising an eyebrow.

"I'm just thinking about yesterday."

Mae's cheeks turned a rosy pink. "Oh," she said, behind a smile she was desperately trying to hide.

"Well, look at the happy couple!" a voice called out behind them.

They turned around and saw Nate and his new wife, Avery, walking toward them. Jonas shook Nate's hand firmly and nodded politely at Avery.

"Nate. Avery. This is my wife, Mae," said Jonas proudly, placing his hand on her lower back.

"It's so nice to meet you," said Mae, shaking their hands.

"Let me see! Let me see!" said Avery, eyeing Mae's left hand.

Mae held it up proudly as the ring sparkled in the stadium lights.

"It's stunning. You did such a good job, Jonas," said Avery.

"Word is, he spent hours with the jeweler," said Nate with a smile. "I was just in Lieberman's yesterday."

Jonas felt Mae glance up at him suddenly. She gave him a curious look before reaching for his hand and interlacing her fingers in his. He closed his fingers around hers comfortably.

"I did. She deserves the best," said Jonas.

"And here I thought you were just like your father." Nate shook his head with a look of surprise.

"I'm full of surprises," said Jonas.

"Well, I'm happy to see that. I was scared to get into business with a robot. Seeing you have a heart makes me know you're the right one to partner with."

Jonas nodded. His plan was working out just as he hoped, and the bonus was Mae.

"Well, I'll let you two go. I know Avery wants to bid on the silent auction." Nate nudged his wife.

"No, I want to bid on the players." She giggled.

Nate rolled his eyes. "I'm going to go broke," he said as she pulled him away.

Jonas and Mae laughed as they waved goodbye. Spotting an opportunity for privacy behind a tent, he pulled Mae behind him.

"What are you—"

He pressed her up against a pillar and pressed his lips against hers. At first, she was surprised, but then he felt her ease against him. She wrapped her arms around his neck and slid her tongue gently against his lips, parting them slightly. He met her tongue eagerly. Hungrily. He grabbed her hips softly before sliding his hands up her jersey and cupping her breasts.

"What's gotten into you?" she whispered between kisses.

"*You*," he said, pressing against her.

She let out a little moan and kissed him again deeply. They heard voices approaching and pulled away quickly. A couple of players rounded the corner, as Jonas slicked back his hair and Mae smoothed out her jersey. Once the players passed, they both burst out laughing.

"You are going to get us in trouble," said Mae, shaking her head.

"You're forgetting I'm the boss."

"And a very hot one at that."

Jonas smiled wide.

"As much as I'd like to stay back here with you. We have to get to work," Mae reminded him.

"Do we have to?" He gave her a puppy dog face.

She laughed as she grabbed his hand and pulled him back out to the festival.

"I'm heading to the balloon pop booth," said Jonas, before kissing her on the cheek.

"I'm working the silent auction. Come find me later."

Jonas watched as she walked away in her skinny jeans and high-top Converse. The girl looked good in anything. And out of it. He smiled to himself as he made his way to his booth. He enjoyed being a part of the festival and having fun with the kids. He loved kids, and up until recently, he didn't see them in his future. But with Mae back in his life, he saw things differently.

He spent the next two hours handing out prizes, replacing the popped balloons, and helping the kids aim their darts. He lifted a little girl up on his shoulders so she could reach better. She giggled with glee as her mom clapped from a distance. When she popped a balloon on her third try, Jonas lowered her to the ground before handing her a giant pink gorilla. She gave him a big hug and skipped away.

"Look at you," said Chad, who sidled up next to him.

"What?" asked Jonas, raising an eyebrow.

"You're, like, ready to be a dad."

Jonas laughed.

"Really. You're like a whole new man." Chad shook his head in disbelief.

Jonas shrugged. "I guess."

"Mae really got to you. I'm happy for you." Chad slapped Jonas on the back.

"Thanks. I'm happy, too."

"Well, maybe I'll find my person during the auction." Chad winked.

Jonas laughed and checked his watch. "It starts soon. We should head over."

He was eager to see his idea come to life. He was also eager to see Mae, who would be working the booth nearby. He saw her from a distance, busy checking her clipboard and happily chatting with patrons. He had a few minutes to go see her.

"I'll see you up there. Good luck," said Jonas, patting Chad's back.

He took a few steps toward Mae's booth, when Nico stepped in front of him. He did not look happy. Annoyed, Jonas rolled his eyes. "What is it, Nico?"

"We haven't finished our conversation about my sister."

Jonas glanced around. Not wanting to make a scene, he gestured toward the back of the stage where the player auction would be held. "Not here."

Nico glared at him before conceding and following him behind the stage. The players mingled about, but when they saw Nico and Jonas, they nervously walked away, giving them some space. Everyone, except Kenny who stayed behind, eyeing them both cautiously.

Jonas leaned against the back steps and looked at Nico coolly. "Can't fight your own, battles?" he asked, nodding at Kenny.

Nico ignored him. "I appreciate you standing up for my sister to that asshole trainer the other day, but I still don't trust you."

"Mae does."

"She's not thinking straight."

"She seemed to be thinking straight just fine yesterday. In my office." Jonas couldn't resist.

Nico took a step toward him, fire burning in his eyes. He raised his hands and shoved Jonas, causing him to stumble backward over the steps. Jonas righted himself and angrily came face to face with Nico. He wanted to hurt him, but not physically.

"It's all fake," said Jonas with a smirk.

"What?" asked Nico, taken aback.

"You heard me. The whole marriage is fake. It was all part of a plan to help me get what I want."

Nico shook his head in shock. "But Mae…why would she agree to that?"

"She'd do anything to protect her baby brother."

Nico looked at him questioningly.

"When I threatened to take your career away, she had no choice but to play along." Jonas shrugged nonchalantly.

"She didn't."

"Of course, she did. I knew exactly how to get to her. So now, I get everything I want. And I get your sister in bed."

Jonas heard a gasp. He whirled around to see Mae standing there with an expression that ripped him clear in two. Tears welled up in her eyes as she tried to hold her focus on Jonas. There was a woman next to her who was holding her children's hands. She looked between him and Mae in utter disbelief.

He took a quick step toward Mae. "Mae—"

"So, none of it is real," whispered Mae, blinking back tears.

"Of course, it is." He reached a hand out for her.

She jerked away from him.

"I can't believe how stupid I've been." She shook her head angrily.

Jonas reached for her again, but her friend stepped in front of her. "Don't." She held up a finger and shook her head.

Mae slowly stepped out from behind her friend, nodding at her reassuringly. She stepped in front of Jonas and pulled her rings off. She pushed them against his chest and he fumbled to grab them as she turned and ran, her friend and her children trailing behind her. He wanted to run after her, but Nico stepped in front of him. Jonas knew what was coming next, but he didn't care. He watched as Nico pulled back his hand and punched him clean in the jaw. Jonas fell to the floor. He watched as Kenny ran over and pulled Nico back before he could land another blow.

He knelt in the dirt, red staining the knees of his jeans. He gripped his face. It hurt, but not nearly as much as it did to watch Mae run away in tears. He feared she would never forgive him. How could he have let his anger get the best of him? It wasn't worth hurting Nico if it broke Mae's heart. He had to find her. He had to make things right.

Chapter 21

Mae

Mae could barely see through her tears as she ran through the festival, desperate to find an exit. Booths and people whirred by her. She really didn't care who saw her in this state. She had to get out of there. Finally, the doors for the exit appeared and she pushed her way through. Outside, she knelt over, placing her hands on her knees, and let out a sob.

She felt so stupid. How could she have trusted him again? How could she have believed he could actually love her? She had been so naïve. As much as she had tried to stay strong and play tough, Jonas had crept into her heart. Or maybe he had been there all this time. She had completely set herself up to be heartbroken. Again.

She heard the doors swing open behind her. She wished for it to be anyone but Jonas.

"When did you become a track star?" asked Lindsay, panting.

Mae whirled around to see her best friend standing there, holding her two kids, red in the face.

"Oh, Lindsay. I'm so sorry. I had to get out of there."

Lindsay waved her off. "Please. You know I've got your back."

"Thank you."

"That man is an asshole." Lindsay wiped a few beads of sweat from her forehead.

"Mom! You can't say that. I'm telling Dad!" her kids yelled.

Lindsay slapped her head against her forehead. "Sorry, loves. Mama did an oopsie."

"You have to put a quarter in the swear jar."

Lindsay rolled her eyes as she set her kids on the ground. She enveloped Mae into a big hug. Mae sunk into her friend as she let more tears flow. Lindsay rubbed her back gently, as her kids came up and clung to Mae's legs.

"It's okay, Aunt Mae," they said, giving her a squeeze.

Mae looked down at them and brushed away her tears. She gave them a forced smile. "Thanks, guys. I'll be okay. I promise." Although, in that moment, she wasn't so sure.

"Can we get out of here?" asked Mae. She knew she shouldn't be leaving work on such a big day, but the event seemed to be running smoothly. Maybe no one would miss her.

"You stay here. I'll go get the car," said Lindsay reassuringly.

Mae nodded as she sat down on the curb with her head in her hands. Lindsay gently grabbed her kids' hands and led them down the sidewalk swiftly.

Mae replayed Jonas's words in her head. *It's all fake. It was all part of a plan. I knew exactly how to get to her.* Mae shook her head, trying to free the words from her memory.

She heard the doors swing open behind her, and this time, she knew it was the one person she couldn't face right now. She could feel Jonas standing behind her. He stayed quiet for what seemed like forever, but was probably only a minute.

"Mae," he said hesitantly.

Mae didn't respond, even though his voice ran through her like liquid. She just stared at the ground. She was scared if she turned and saw him, she would somehow forget the awful things he said and end up in his arms. Like an idiot. Again.

She heard him take a few slow steps toward her. Mae lifted her head from her hands and blinked back tears. She didn't want him to see her like this. Taking a deep breath, Mae stared straight ahead. She felt Jonas gently place his hand on her shoulder. Flinching at his touch, she stood up quickly.

"Don't," said Mae sharply, turning around and bravely meeting his gaze. "Don't touch me."

Jonas pulled his hand back slowly and looked down at his feet. "What you heard back there—"

"Which part? That you knew *exactly* how to get to me? Or that it was all fake?"

"I didn't mean for you to hear that." Jonas winced.

"Well, I did."

"I didn't mean it. You have to know that."

"I don't know anything when it comes to you. I don't know up from down or left from right. I don't know what's wrong or right. And I sure as hell don't know what's real and what's fake."

"If you would just let me explain."

"How many chances do I have to give you, Jonas?"

He looked at her sadly, but she quickly avoided his gaze. She would not get sucked into this again. They stood in silence for a few moments until they heard a squeal of a car turning the corner. Lindsay pulled up to the curb and opened the passenger door. "Get in."

Mae was so grateful for her friend in that moment. She didn't hesitate as she slid into the seat, shutting the door and looking straight ahead. "Drive."

"Seatbelt," said Lindsay as she pressed on the gas.

Mae clicked her seatbelt into place and resisted looking in the mirror. She didn't have to look. She knew he was watching them drive away until they were out of sight. Eyes closed, she laid her head against the cool window, and tried her best not to cry.

"We're here," said Lindsay softly as she gently shook Mae.

Mae lifted her head from the window groggily. She had fallen asleep. She blinked a few times and saw they were pulling into Lindsay's driveway. This was exactly where she wanted to be. In the suburbs and far away from the city. She felt guilty that she hadn't been here in years. She nodded as she unbuckled her seatbelt and got out of the car sleepily.

Lindsay opened the front door and her kids pushed their way inside.

"Daddy! We're home!" they shouted as they started to run upstairs. A loud monster growl sounded as Ben appeared at the top of the stairs. The kids giggled with delight and gave him a huge bear hug.

Lindsay smiled up at him. "Mae's here!"

Mae stepped inside and gave a little wave.

"Well, I'll be! It's been ages," said Ben as he wrestled the kids off him.

He climbed down the stairs and gave Mae a big hug.

"How the heck have you been? How's work? How's Nico? How's everything?" he asked eagerly.

"As much as Mae would like to give you her entire life story, we need a little girl time. Can you occupy Thing 1 and Thing 2?" Lindsay nodded up the stairs to where Ellie and Jack were sitting.

Ben gave a little salute. "You've got it." He headed up the stairs and threw the kids over his shoulders, carrying them out of sight.

Mae couldn't help but feel a little pang in her heart. Lindsay and Ben made such a good team. Their house was filled with love and they were living their dream. Mae wondered if it was too late for her. Maybe she had pined after Jonas for too long and had missed out on real love.

"Come on. Sit." Lindsay gestured to the couch before heading into the kitchen.

Mae collapsed on the couch and let out a sigh. She was emotionally drained. Lindsay handed her a water and took the seat beside her, tucking her feet underneath her.

"How are you feeling, hun?" she asked.

"I'm feeling like an idiot. You heard what he said back there."

"I wish I hadn't. But did you see the punch Nico got in? That was impressive."

Mae shook her head. "What a mess. I guess now is when you say 'I told you so.'"

Lindsay shook her head. "This is not something I wanted to be right about. Trust me. I saw you two at the festival. You looked totally in love or at least somewhere close."

"He had everyone fooled, including me."

"I don't know. He'd have to be a pretty good actor to look at you that way."

"How could he say those awful things then?"

Lindsay shrugged. "I don't know what to tell you, Mae."

Mae looked at her friend for a moment. Her friend, who took care of her with no judgment whatsoever and got her out of a bad situation with the man she had warned her about. Mae felt guilt wash over her.

"Am I a bad friend?" Mae asked suddenly.

"What? Where did *that* come from?"

"I haven't been here in years. I barely see you. Or the kids. Or Ben."

"You've been busy. It's okay."

"It's *not* okay. I've been working at a job I'm not even sure I love to be close to my brother—who probably needs to grow up."

"Oh, he definitely needs to grow up." Lindsay laughed softly before she looked at Mae seriously. "You're the hardest working person I know. Whether you love the job or not, you've proven yourself to be a valuable asset. And if you don't love it, then quit. Anyone would be lucky to have you."

Mae thought about the idea of no longer working at the only job she'd really ever known. What would it feel like stepping away from the role of Nico's mother, and just be his sister? His friend. She also thought about the idea of not seeing Jonas every day. As much as she had avoided him since their breakup, she still felt her heart drop whenever she saw him.

"But I've also been gallivanting around with someone I thought would eventually love me. I could have left years ago when he broke my heart the first time. Why did I stick around? It's like I wanted to torture myself." Mae shook her head, frustrated with herself.

"Mae." Lindsay grabbed her hand and gave it a squeeze. Mae looked up at her, fighting back tears.

"Sure, maybe you're a little blind when it comes to Jonas. But sometimes you have to make mistakes. It's how you learn," said Lindsay.

"I should have learned the first time."

"Ahh woulda, coulda, shoulda." Lindsay waved her off. "We've been best friends for years. Nothing is going to change that. You've seen me at my worst, and I've seen you at yours. You're stuck with me."

Mae hugged Lindsay tightly. "Thank you."

She heard someone clear their throat. They looked up to see Ben in the doorway, rocking on his heels awkwardly. "I got a little hungry, so I set the kids up with a movie so I could grab a bite from the kitchen. Is girl time over?"

Lindsay rolled her eyes. "I'll heat up some leftovers. Are you hungry, Mae?"

Mae shook her head no. She watched as her friend playfully shoved Ben toward the kitchen. She let out a little laugh and looked up at the ceiling.

A moment later, Ben plopped down next to her on the couch with two beers in hand. He nudged her gently.

"You want one?"

"Yes, please," said Mae, taking one.

They clinked their bottles together and took a big swig.

"Thanks, Ben. I needed that."

"I heard."

Mae looked at him and raised an eyebrow.

"I might have eavesdropped a little." Ben shrugged.

"Is my drama entertaining?" Mae held back a smile.

"I'm a doorknob salesman and I live in the suburbs. What do you think?"

Mae laughed out loud.

"Glad I could help."

Lindsay walked in holding a beer and sat down next to them on the couch. "Sounds like someone is feeling better." She clinked her bottle against Mae's and winked.

It was true. Mae did feel better. Her heart was still shattered into a million pieces, but being with the people who knew her inside and out helped. This house helped. It reminded her of her parents' house, which wasn't far away. It wasn't until now that she realized how much she missed it. How much she missed her brother. Maybe some time away from the city would be good for her.

"Can I stay here with you? Just for a little while?" she asked, looking from Ben to Lindsay.

"Stay as long as you'd like," said Lindsay.

Chapter 22

Jonas

After he watched Mae drive away, Jonas tried calling her several times, but she ignored his calls and eventually must have turned off her phone because it went straight to voicemail. He had no idea where she was headed or who was driving. He felt completely helpless. He also felt like an asshole.

How could he have said those things? They weren't even true. He was just in the heat of the moment. Jonas walked defeatedly headed back into the festival. He hoped Mae could understand. Someday.

Despite what just happened, he still had a company to run. When this was over, he promised he would find her and make things right. He straightened his jacket and headed back through the doors to the festival. Braydon stood at a nearby booth, pacing anxiously. When he spotted Jonas, he made a beeline toward him.

"There you are! We've been looking for you!"

"Sorry, I had to...deal with something."

"Jesus, look at your eye. It's already starting to bruise."

Jonas touched his face and winced. It was tender from where Nico had punched him.

"You should really get some ice on that," said Braydon, leading him to a booth.

"Can we get a bag of ice?" Braydon asked the girl running the booth. She nodded nervously, looking at Jonas, and prepared a bag. She handed it to him.

"Thank you," said Jonas, taking it from her.

"Let's put that ice on you behind the stage. We don't want any more people asking questions," said Braydon, looking around nervously.

"How bad is it?" asked Jonas as they walked swiftly toward the stage.

"Thankfully, no patrons saw what happened because you were hidden behind the stage. But the team is asking questions. Chad found me right after the altercation with Nico. Do you mind telling me what the hell is going on?"

"It was about Mae."

Braydon nodded. "Well, you better sort it out."

Jonas was glad that the public hadn't witnessed the scene. He didn't need that kind of media attention, especially here at the festival. It would not be a good look for a charity fundraiser. He followed Braydon behind the stage where the team was waiting, including Nico, who eyed him warily.

Jonas cleared his throat and the team stood a little taller as they eagerly waited to hear what he had to say.

"I want to apologize for what happened today. It was unprofessional and I assure you it won't happen again. Isn't that right, Nico?" Jonas shot Nico a sharp look.

He nodded sheepishly. "Yes, sir. Sorry, guys."

"Now, I want you all up on that stage looking like prizes. Let's forget the drama and raise some money for the kids."

The team whooped in agreement.

"You can let the emcee know we are ready to start the auction," Jonas said to Braydon.

Braydon nodded as he walked up the steps of the stage to the sound booth.

Moments later, the players were announced one by one. Jonas heard the crowd go wild with cheers and was happy to hear the amounts shouted out. A few players were waiting by the steps to be called. Jonas spotted Nico and walked over.

Nico looked him up and down as he approached. "I'm not apologizing to you," he said.

"Look, Nico, as much as I would like to kick your ass off the team, you're under contract. I'd have to jump through quite a few hoops to make that happen, and it's not high on my priority list at the moment. But if you ever lay your hands on me again, I can make it a priority."

Nico remained silent.

"If you can't respect me, at least be respectful of the team. Of the sport. Of my father's legacy."

At that, Nico looked at him and nodded slowly. "Okay."

Nico's name was called up to the stage and the crowd really went wild. He was a fan favorite. There was no denying that. Jonas really hoped they could put this behind them. He sat on the steps, holding ice to his eye. He didn't want anyone to see him like this and make any speculations. Jonas listened as the bids grew higher and higher. Nico was auctioned off for $11,000. The highest of the day.

The players excitedly clambered down the stairs, slapping each other on the back proudly. Jonas stood and shook their hands.

"That was some auction. This will undoubtedly go down as the highest profiting charity event we've ever had. Thanks, boys."

239

They whooped and hollered, and began chatting animatedly about who they were auctioned off to.

"Did you see the blonde cougar who bid on me? Those things can't be real," said Chad.

"I got someone my grandma's age," said Kenny warily.

"Nico, you lucked out with that brunette," said Chad, slapping him on the back.

"Right? She didn't have to pay me to take her out. I would have done it for free." Nico winked.

Jonas forced a smile as he listened to their banter, but internally he was only thinking about Mae. He kept telling himself that if he could just talk to her again, she would understand. Even though he said it, his mind was a traitor that wouldn't allow him to believe it. He knew he had broken her heart all those years ago. It had been a mistake then, and it was a mistake now. How many chances was she really willing to give him?

"Why the long face?" Braydon put an arm around him.

"Just tired," Jonas lied.

Braydon looked at him knowingly. "You should go find her."

"But the festival…"

"I can handle it from here. It's almost over, anyway. Plus, you heard the auction. This is our most successful festival yet. Your dad would be proud."

Jonas shrugged. "I don't know about that."

"Well, *I'm* proud of you, Jonas. Now go." Braydon gave him a little shove.

Jonas smiled at him before quickly finding the exit. He called his driver, who met him where Mae had left him earlier. He tried calling Mae as he slid into the backseat. Her phone was still off. He sighed frustratedly.

"Where to, Mr. Matthews?" asked his driver, looking back in the rearview mirror.

Jonas thought for a moment. Maybe she was at his place. Not to stay, but probably packing her things.

"Home, please."

Jonas tapped his foot impatiently as they drove and as he rode up the elevator to his place. He hoped he wasn't too late. He quickly unlocked his door and stepped inside.

"Mae?" he called out.

There was no answer. He looked around the condo, but everything was as he left it. He walked down the hallway to her room and pushed the door open to see all of her things still there. Jonas breathed a small sigh of relief, but was disappointed she wasn't there. He sat down on the edge of her bed and looked around solemnly. Her perfume still lingered in the air and he breathed in as he put his head in his hands. Where could she be?

He thought for a moment before opening the drawer of her nightstand. It didn't feel right to go through her things, but he was looking for a clue of where she could be. He found an address book and excitedly flipped through it. After a few pages he realized it was no use. There were so many contacts, and many of them were business contacts. He couldn't call every single one.

Frustrated, he shut the book and went to put it back in the drawer. Just as he was about to shut it, he spotted the corner of a picture peeking out. He slid it out from underneath the romance books she loved to read and smiled when he realized what it was.

It was a picture of them. Probably the only one they had together. He had taken it in his old apartment. Her head laid on his shoulder as they sat on the couch. He had made a funny face by crossing his eyes and sticking his tongue out. She was laughing in the picture. Her nose scrunched up and all her teeth showed. Jonas could hear it now. He loved her laugh.

Jonas stood from the bed, desperate to find her. He wouldn't give up. He couldn't lose her. He tried the office, but it was empty. Everyone was at the festival. He tried the corner market where she would stop for wine, but the owner hadn't seen her. He tried her favorite coffee shop, but she wasn't there. Jonas walked defeatedly back to the car and closed the door behind him. His driver looked at him questioningly.

Out of options, Jonas thought of one more place she might be, and it was the last place he wanted to go. He looked through his contacts and found the address he needed, and gave it to his driver. A short drive later, he got out of the car and walked into the apartment building. He skipped the elevator and walked up the two flights of stairs swiftly. When he reached the door, he knocked and waited with bated breath.

He heard the door unlock and watched it open to Nico standing in the doorway. He looked at Jonas, surprised.

"What the hell do you want?" he asked, keeping his hand on the door.

"Please, Nico. Is she here?"

"Who?"

"Don't play dumb."

Nico sighed. "She's not here."

Jonas didn't believe him. He pushed through the door and entered Nico's apartment.

"Are you serious right now?" asked Nico. "I told you she's not here."

Jonas glanced around, hoping for a sign Mae was there or had been there. Another player named Josh walked into the living room. He looked at Jonas, confused.

"Hey, boss." He eyed Jonas and Nico warily. "I'm not going to have to break up another fight, am I?"

"No, no. Everything is fine, Josh," Jonas assured him. "Actually, can you give us a moment?"

Josh nodded. He gave Nico a questioning look as he grabbed a beer from the fridge. Nico nodded an *it's okay* and Josh headed back down the hall to his room. He didn't shut the door all the way and Jonas was pretty sure he was eavesdropping, but he didn't care.

"Look, Nico. I know we have our history," said Jonas.

"Yeah, but I don't know why."

"You really don't know?"

"No. You've just hated me from the beginning. I've never done anything to you."

Jonas sighed. If he were to win Mae back, it was time he was honest. Not only with her, but the people who mattered to her.

"May I sit?" Jonas gestured toward the couch.

"Sure." Nico slowly sat down on the opposite end as Jonas took a seat.

"It was never anything *you* did. It was really about my father and his infatuation with you. I worked my whole life to be noticed by him, and you just waltzed in, fresh out of college, and he took to you quickly. I hated you for it."

"Wow." Nico looked surprised.

"Yeah, now you know."

"But your father talked about you all the time," said Nico.

Jonas looked at him skeptically.

"It's true. He was proud of you."

"He had a funny way of showing it." Jonas looked down at his hands.

"I don't know much about father-son relationships because…Well, you know. But I would think he wouldn't want you to dwell on the past."

"What are you? My therapist now?" asked Jonas, amused.

Nico laughed. Jonas couldn't help but smile.

"I'm sorry about the shiner." Nico nodded to Jonas's eye.

"I'll forgive you if you tell me where your sister is."

Nico sighed. "You really won't let up, will you?"

Jonas shook his head.

"Well, I really don't know where she is. And that's the truth."

Jonas believed him. Frustrated at not being any closer to finding Mae, he went home.

Chapter 23

Mae

Mae rolled over in the twin-sized bed and watched the sun rise as it peeked through the curtains. She had slept surprisingly well for sleeping in a toddler's bed, fit with unicorn sheets and pink, frilly pillows. She rubbed her eyes as she sat up in bed and wondered if today would hurt any less than the past few had. But no. The pain trickled in as soon as she woke up and grew into a large mass that pooled around her heart.

She shut her eyes tight, willing the tears back. Her chest hurt as she tried to hold in a small sob. It had been two days since the festival. Two days since her heart had been shattered. Again. By the same man she'd loved all these years, despite breaking her heart. Twice.

The many faces of Jonas popped into her head and played like a slideshow. There was his morning face that pissed her off because he was an early bird, and she needed an IV of coffee. There was his business face that was serious, but also maybe a little unsure of himself. There was his laughing face that was lit by the reality show on the television. There was his face when they made love, his eyes locked on hers, like he was fully there in that moment.

Mae shook her head, trying to scatter the memories so they wouldn't form together again and work against her. She smelled coffee coming from the kitchen. She had no idea what time it was. She went to check her phone, but it was off. It had been off since she drove away from Jonas. She didn't want to hear from him. She couldn't hear his voice.

"Oh, good. You're up," said Lindsay, peeking into the room.

"What time is it?" asked Mae.

"It's just after ten."

"Oh, my gosh. I'm sorry!"

"What are you sorry for? You deserve the rest."

"I haven't slept in like this since college." Mae laughed.

"Yeah. Those frat parties were no joke." Lindsay shuddered.

Mae laughed.

"Can Ellie come in and grab her unicorn?" Lindsay asked as her daughter peeped her head in the doorway.

"Of course she can! I'm sorry, Ellie," said Mae.

"Thanks, Aunt Mae," said the little girl as she skipped into her room.

"You probably want your room back, huh?"

"No! I want you to stay here forever!" Ellie gave her a big hug.

Mae smiled down at her. As much as she would like to stay here forever, she knew eventually she had to face the music. Just not today.

Ellie began playing in her room while Mae followed Lindsay downstairs. She took a seat at the counter and Lindsay handed her a hot cup of coffee.

"How are you feeling?" asked Lindsay.

"Better-ish." Mae let out a sigh. "That's a lie. I'm still totally hurt. Shocked. Pissed."

"All valid feelings." Lindsay took a sip of coffee.

"Being here helps. I realize how much I missed living away from the city. I feel closer to Mom and Dad out here."

Lindsay nodded. "I miss them."

"Me too."

Mae and Lindsay had grown up together. They would always stay at each other's houses for sleepovers or campouts. They were in dance together. They were in the same classes at school. They went to the same college. Mae had been her maid of honor at her wedding. Lindsay was like her sister and her parents treated her as such. When they had passed away, Lindsay had stayed with Mae for months to help her cope. Now here she was, coming to her rescue again.

"Thank you," said Mae. "For everything."

"Of course." Lindsay reached for her hand and gave it a squeeze.

Ben came through the front door holding bags of groceries. "Breakfast, anyone?"

Mae hopped off the stool and helped unbag the groceries while he fired up the stove. Soon the kitchen smelled of eggs, bacon, and buttermilk pancakes. Ellie and Jack flew down the stairs.

"Pancakes!" they exclaimed as they sat down at the dining table.

Lindsay began setting the table while Ben started filling plates up with food. As good as everything smelled, Mae didn't feel that hungry. She had barely eaten anything since she had been here. She knew this was Ben's kind gesture of trying to take care of her. It made her so happy her friend had a good man in her life.

"I'm just going to make a quick phone call. Please start without me," said Mae. She walked up the stairs to Ellie's room and looked through her purse for her phone. She powered it on and scrolled through her contacts to Braydon. She hit send and listened to the lull of rings.

"Mae! There you are!"

"Hi, Braydon. I'm so sorry I went MIA."

"I was worried about you. Where are you?" he asked.

"I'm with an old friend. I just needed some time away."

"Does this have to do with Jonas? Is that why you're avoiding the office?"

Mae remained silent. She wasn't ready to talk about it, especially not with Braydon. He had loved the idea of them together. He was also like her second father. She would hate to disappoint him.

"I know there was some drama at the festival. Now, I don't know what it was about, but, Mae. Let me tell you something about love. Love is wild, my dear. You don't let it go after one fight."

Mae stifled a laugh. If only Braydon knew that this wasn't the first time. There was no point in telling him. It wouldn't change anything. In fact, she was positive it would only make her seem like a fool.

"Sorry, I know it's none of my business. I just loved the two of you together, but I love *you* more. You know what's best."

"I will probably be out for a few more days. Is that okay?"

"Of course. Now that the festival is over, things are starting to slow down around here. All we have is the gala tonight, but that's just a party to schmooze over champagne."

"Thank you, Braydon. Truly. I appreciate it."

"Call if you need anything, Mae."

She hung up and turned her phone off again before heading downstairs to eat breakfast.

"All good?" asked Lindsay, raising an eyebrow.

"Yeah. I figured it was time to call my boss before he fired me."

"Braydon? That man would never fire you. I think he'd adopt you if he could." Lindsay laughed.

Ben set down a plate of pancakes with two eggs for eyes and bacon for a mouth. Mae looked at it and giggled. It was the first time she had smiled in days.

"I think it's going to be my last night here," she said in between bites.

"No!" Ellie shouted. "Who will keep my bed warm?"

"You, silly," said Mae with a smile.

"But where will you go?" asked Lindsay, concerned.

"I'll get a hotel for a little while until I figure things out."

"Like hell you will," said Ben with a mouthful of bacon.

"Or I'll stay with Nico for a little while. It's time we finally talked," said Mae, assuring. "I can't stay here forever."

"You can, but I *do* like the idea of you patching things up with your brother," said Lindsay.

Mae nodded in agreement. She truly missed her brother. They had gone from living together, to living apart, to not speaking. It just wasn't natural. She felt like a piece of her was missing. She promised herself she would text her brother later that evening.

The next day, Mae took a long shower and got dressed. Since she didn't have any of her things, she had been borrowing clothes from Lindsay. Thankfully, they were the same size. She slid on a pair of jeans and a sweater. She looked in the mirror and was happy to see her eyes weren't giant, red, puffy pillows anymore.

Downstairs, she hugged Ellie and Jack goodbye. "I promise I will be around more."

And she meant it. Having this time with her best friend and her family made her realize what her priorities had been for years, and where they should be.

Ben gave her a hug. "Don't be a stranger."

"I won't."

She followed Lindsay into the garage and slid into the passenger seat. The drive to Jonas's went by too fast, and soon, Lindsay was parked at the curb.

"Are you ready for this?" she asked, eyeing Mae.

"He's not home. There is a work gala tonight. Braydon reminded me earlier. I'll be in and out."

Lindsay nodded, as if comforted by the thought.

"Do you want me to come up?"

"No, no. You've done enough. I'm fine." Mae waved her off before giving her a big hug.

"I'll see you soon, okay?" whispered Lindsay.

Mae kissed her on the cheek and climbed out of the car. It felt weird being back in the building, knowing it wasn't her home anymore. Knowing that Jonas would still be here, carrying on with his life as if she was just a blip. She swallowed hard thinking about it, as she pressed the button for the elevator and rode numbly to the top floor.

She unlocked the door and stepped inside. The lights were off, but the fireplace was on.

That's strange, she thought. Maybe he had forgotten to turn it off. She went to flip the switch when she heard Jonas's voice cut through the silence.

"You came back."

She followed the voice and saw him sitting on the couch. He wore a suit, but his tie and the buttons were undone. His hair was a mess and he looked disheveled.

"What are you doing here?" she asked, trying to keep her voice from trembling. "I thought the gala was tonight."

"It is," he said, standing up and taking a step towards her. "I wanted to be here in case you came back."

"I'm not back, Jonas. I'm just here to get my things." Mae set her purse down and started toward the hallway to her room.

"Mae, please," he called, but she ignored him.

Once she was in her room, she shut the door and locked it before her knees gave out and she slid down the length of her door. Mae put her head in her hands and took a few deep breaths. She had never seen anyone look so sad. He was a mess. Had he really missed out on a work event to wait for her? That wasn't like him.

She pushed those thoughts from her head and focused on what she was here to do. She began packing her suitcase. She wouldn't be able to take everything tonight, not with him just down the hall. She would just pack the necessities and wait for Nico at his apartment. Once her bag was packed, she opened her bedroom door and walked toward the living room.

The lights were on and Jonas was leaning against the couch, waiting for her. He eyed her suitcase.

"I'll come back and get the rest of my stuff another day," said Mae as she walked past him.

"Please don't go, Mae."

"You got what you wanted, Jonas. You got your deal with Nate. You got people to think you had a heart. You don't need me anymore. This façade is over. We are done."

He looked at her intently and grabbed her hand, pulling her toward him. "We aren't done. Not even close." The next thing she knew, his lips were pressed against hers and her heart betrayed her head. She pulled back and looked up at him with tears in her eyes.

"You have to listen to me," he said, pressing his forehead against hers. "Please."

Mae slowly nodded and reluctantly took a seat on the couch. She told herself this would be the closure they needed. She was lying.

Chapter 24

Jonas

As much as Jonas wanted Mae to walk through the door, it completely took him off guard when she did. His hope had started to dwindle after so many calls and so much searching, and no sign of her. When he heard the key in the door, he thought he was imagining it. She was the only person who had a key.

He was glad he had not gone to the gala. Jonas had gotten dressed in his tux and was ready to call his driver when he decided not to go at the last minute. He couldn't be in a crowd of people pretending everything was fine. Plastering on a smile as if his world wasn't caving in on itself. He definitely wasn't in the mood to see Nico either. Although they seemed to leave things on good terms at his apartment, he was just another reminder of Mae.

Jonas had called Wendy first, and then Braydon. He told both he was feeling under the weather. Wendy didn't ask questions and had chicken noodle soup delivered. Braydon was a different story.

"A sick day, huh?" Braydon had asked skeptically over the phone.

"That's right," said Jonas. His energy was low, he didn't even have to fake it.

"In the ten years you've been with the company, I can count your days off on one hand."

Jonas sighed for effect. "I hate to miss the gala, but I've come down with something."

"I hear that's going around. My assistant is out with it, too. Haven't seen her in days. The doctors are saying it's something called… heartbreak."

Jonas rolled his eyes so hard, he was sure Braydon could hear it through the line. He was happy to hear any news on Mae, although it meant she was hurting and gave him no clues as to where she was.

But now here she was. Sitting on his couch. He didn't know how long he had. He had to get this right. Jonas started to pace the living room, while trying to find the words to say to her. He could barely look at her. He knew she was trying to keep calm, play it cool, icy even. But he could see the sadness in her eyes that failed to meet his. And he hated himself for putting that sadness inside her.

She looked so beautiful. Despite everything she was going through. Seeing her sitting there made his heart long for her, and she was right in front of him. He missed her already. If he missed her this much when she was a few feet away, how would it be if she left his life for good?

Finally, Jonas stopped pacing and leaned against the mantle of the fireplace with his back to her. The only way he could start was if he was not staring straight at the beautiful woman who wanted to be anywhere else but here. Understandably so.

"What I said to your brother the other day…it wasn't true." He looked down at the fireplace.

"Then why say it?"

"It was in the moment. I was heated. I just wanted to get under his skin. Piss him off. You know? It's no excuse, but it's the truth."

"Why the hell do you hate him so much?" asked Mae frustratedly.

Jonas sighed and shook his head. Mae waited for him to speak. He turned around, but didn't meet her questioning gaze. Instead, he looked out at the city contemplatively.

"Did you know my father almost left the team to Nico? His entire company?" he asked softly.

"What? What are you talking about?" she asked, surprised.

"Yeah. I saw the papers drawn up on his desk one day. It was right after he got sick. He knew he didn't have much time left, so I guess he wanted to make changes to his will."

"Maybe you read it wrong."

"I read it three times to make sure I was understanding correctly. I didn't read it wrong. He was going to leave his entire legacy to your brother. A twenty-three-year-old kid."

"But why? Why Nico?" She sounded genuinely confused.

Jonas shrugged. He thought she would have some insight into their relationship, but she seemed just as lost as he was.

"It was no surprise to anyone that my father took to your brother almost immediately," Jonas continued.

Mae nodded.

"I spent years trying to understand it. Was it because he was the underdog? Was it because it was somewhat of a Cinderella story? Was it because he felt obligated to be a father figure to him?"

Jonas was pouring it all out. He had never opened up to anyone about the relationship with his father, or the lack thereof. He especially never opened up about how much it had ravaged him internally.

"I knew they were close, but not to where he'd leave Nico his company. I know for a fact Nico had no idea about any of this."

This gave Jonas some piece of mind. Maybe no one knew the inner workings of his father's mind.

"In the end, he didn't. Obviously. I don't know what made him choose me."

"You're his *son,* Jonas."

Jonas let out a laugh. "His son," he repeated to himself. "He sure as hell didn't act like it. When I was younger, I would wake up early to catch him before he went to work, and all I got was a nod on his way out the door. My bedtime was before he even clocked out of the office, even though I begged my mom to let me stay up. She always assured me he would come check on me when he got home from work. I stayed up enough nights to know he never even walked down the hallway to my room."

Mae looked at him sympathetically. He didn't want her to feel bad for him. He just wanted her to understand.

He continued, "I just wanted to be close to him. That's why I wanted to work at the company after college. To be close to him. He made me go through several interview processes, and wouldn't even meet with me himself. Maybe it was to show there was no favoritism. But damn, it was the exact opposite. Even when I became his employee, that's all I was to him. I tried everything to be the man he wanted me to be. Hell, the child he wanted me to be. But nothing was ever good enough."

"I had no idea, Jonas. I mean, I knew how hard you worked, but I didn't know why, until now," said Mae softly. "You never told me any of this."

"I was too embarrassed. What father doesn't love their son?"

"He loved you, Jonas. He probably just didn't know how to show it."

"He loved work. No matter what I did, I always came second to it. Second to the team. Then your brother came into the picture."

"And you fell even further down the ladder."

Jonas nodded. "I just wanted Nico to know what it felt like to come second to the person he loved the most."

Mae thought for a moment. "By using me in the process," she said coldly.

"I know what I asked you to do wasn't right. I see that now. Hell, I saw it when I proposed the idea."

"Proposed? More like blackmailed."

"I wasn't thinking straight. I was so focused on getting back at Nico that I didn't care about anything else."

"Or any*one*."

Jonas could see her walls were still high and he wondered if he were getting any closer to knocking them down. It was actually more like a steep climb to the top, and he was terrified of what was over the edge.

"Why *did* you choose me? *Really?*"

"Because it's *you*."

She looked at him curiously.

"Aside from the nasty way I went about it, I knew deep down it meant spending time with you." Jonas sighed. "The truth is, I've missed you."

Mae remained silent.

"I've missed you since I let you leave my apartment all those years ago."

"But you let me leave. You didn't fight for me. For us. You're the one who ended things."

"And I've regretted it every day. I was a stupid kid back then. Trying to make it in the big world.

Trying to live up to his father's absurd expectations."

"You hurt me, Jonas," she said softly.

Jonas took a slow step toward her. "I know."

"Twice."

"I know."

Mae seemed to gather her strength and stood slowly from the couch. She shook her head.

"Look, I appreciate you telling me the truth. I know that wasn't easy for you. But it's all too little too late, Jonas."

She took a few steps toward the door before Jonas gently grabbed her hand. She looked at his hand enclosed around hers and slowly up at him. "You know I can't do this again."

Her words hit him like a punch to the gut. He held onto her hand like a life raft. Because surely if she left again, he would drown. She didn't pull away. Not yet, at least. He studied her face, but he couldn't read her. It was a pool of anger, sadness, regret, fear.

"I'm here, Mae. For good."

"I wish I could believe that."

"You can," he said assuredly.

"How am I supposed to trust you? Again?"

"I don't know, but I'll spend every day proving that you can. I want to be with you."

"But you told Nico it was all fake."

"I was stupid. I'm so sorry. I didn't mean it."

She furrowed her brow, not believing him. He took her head between his hands and brought his forehead to meet hers. He felt her suck in a breath. Every memory they had together flooded back to him.

"I'm *ready*. I'm ready for all of it. I'm ready to be home at 5:30 every day. I'm ready to eat Chinese food on the couch and watch those awful dating shows. I'm ready to deal with your grumpy ass in the mornings when an IV of coffee wouldn't be able to lift your mood. I'm ready to enjoy a glass of wine with you and watch the sunset every evening. I'm ready to lie with you in bed, tangled in the sheets. I'm ready to be your husband."

She looked up at him through her lashes and bit her bottom lip, still unsure. He brushed his thumb against her lip softly and knelt down to kiss her. She didn't pull away, but she didn't fully let go. How could he convince her? Then he thought of it. He felt for his back pocket. The ring.

After she had pushed it at him at the festival, he had dropped it. He spent several moments frantically searching for it in the grass. It wasn't about the ring. It was about what it meant. It was about who it belonged with. That person was Mae. Afraid of losing it again, he kept it with him.

He knelt down on one knee, pulling the ring from his pocket. She put her hand to her mouth and gasped as she looked down at him. This time, it was real.

"You're it for me, Mae. You always have been."

She shook her head in disbelief.

"I love you so much. Will you marry me?" he asked. Every bit of hope he had was doing cartwheels in his stomach as he waited for her answer.

After what felt like an eternity, she nodded slowly, holding back a smile.

She stared down at him for a moment before giving him her hand. "Only if it's for real this time."

"It's real. It's so real." He placed the ring on her finger.

She knelt down to kiss him softly before pulling away and looking at the ring sparkling on her hand. "Now, I've been meaning to ask. Is *this* real?" She wiggled her fingers at him and Jonas laughed. He pulled her in for another kiss. Taking her by surprise, they tumbled to the floor laughing.

Epilogue

Mae

Mae pulled into the garage as she watched the sunset in the rearview mirror. She smiled at Jonas's car that was already parked next to hers. She checked the time on the dash before turning the car off. It was 5:30 p.m. He beat her again. Ever since he had challenged himself to leave the office on time, he had never been late. It had been a year, and he was always been home before her. Mae loved that about him.

She switched off the ignition and grabbed her purse from the front seat. She saw her phone light up with a notification. It was a text from Nico:

Threw my fastest pitch at training today!

Mae smiled and texted back: *So proud of you!*

She was so happy they had patched things up after all the drama. Jonas was the one who had forced them to meet for dinner and hash everything out. He had tricked them both into it because they both probably would have been too stubborn. He had told Mae he had made a dinner reservation for a date, and he had Braydon tell Nico it was a business meeting.

When Mae showed up at the restaurant, the hostess led her to a table where an unsuspecting Nico sat. After a few awkward minutes, they ordered a bottle of wine, and finally talked about everything. Mae explained everything about Jonas, and although Nico didn't warm up to the idea of them together right away, he'd finally come to terms with it. He even texted Jonas sometimes. What they talked about, Mae had no idea, but she was happy. The two men she loved finally got along.

She clicked off her phone and slid it into her purse before heading inside. She was met with the smell of garlic and spices wafting in the air. Her stomach grumbled loudly. She set her things down on the entry table and walked quietly through the house. Their house. She ran her fingers lovingly against the wall as she made her way to the kitchen.

They had moved to the suburbs a few months ago. Ever since she had stayed at Lindsay's during that emotional time she'd rather forget, Mae realized how much she missed the home she grew up in. She missed the tree-lined streets, cul-desacs, and the quietness of a small neighborhood. It felt like a piece of her was missing in the city.

She thought she would have to talk Jonas into it, but he was happy to leave the city. He had said he wanted a fresh start with her. After he had proposed to her a second time, they had a small courthouse wedding to make everything *real*. They had never smiled so big as they did in that courthouse in front of the judge. Their cheeks actually hurt.

Afterward, they popped champagne in the back of his town car, which unbeknownst to her was driving away from the city. When the car stopped and Mae finally came up for air from kissing her husband (for real), she realized they were in front of a charming two-story Colonial. Confused, she looked at Jonas for answers, but he just had a secretive smile on his face.

"Welcome home, wife."

She gasped as she pressed her hands against the window and gawked at the house. It was perfect, with white shutters and a wrap-around porch. There were rose bushes growing neatly on the lawn. Children riding bikes whizzed by on the sidewalk laughing.

"Jonas. What did you do?" asked Mae slowly.

"Do you like it?" He grabbed her hand and gave it a squeeze.

She felt her eyes tear up as she squeezed his hand back. It was perfect. It reminded her so much of her childhood home.

"I love it."

Now, she leaned against the wall of the entryway to the kitchen and admired her husband. She still couldn't wrap her head around the idea. Jonas had music playing and hadn't heard her come in. She stayed quiet and took it all in. He was wearing the gray sweats she loved and a fitted white t-shirt as he moved confidently around the kitchen. The cooking classes they had taken together last month were paying off. She hadn't cooked in weeks, which she was grateful for. She had been so busy at her new job.

When Braydon retired shortly after the festival, she felt like it was the right time to try something new. She also felt like it was time to give Nico the space to grow and come into his own, without his big sister always around. When she told him, he was disappointed at first. Maybe even a little scared, but in the end, he understood.

He now lived in a high-rise apartment with his best friend and teammate, Kenny. They were both living the bachelor life, although Kenny seemed to be a good influence on Nico. Mae was thankful for that.

When she put in her two weeks' notice, she started looking around for different jobs. She still wanted to be in the industry that she knew so well, and that her parents had been immersed in. It made her feel close to them.

Everything seemed to line up when Jonas casually mentioned her career change to Nate. Nate was looking for someone to head up the athletic line he and Jonas were launching. She excitedly accepted the job and had been building everything from the ground up ever since. It was new and challenging, but she was proud of herself. Plus, she got to see Jonas still. Jonas split his time between offices. She still got giddy when she saw him walk in her office. Now they didn't have to hide anything.

She watched as Jonas danced to the music and added some salt to the pan. He shook his butt and she couldn't help but laugh. He whipped around in surprise and smiled when he saw her. His cheeks turned a rosy pink.

"Those were some moves," said Mae, wiggling her eyebrows.

"You haven't seen nothin' yet." He danced toward her and wrapped his arms around her. She let out a comforted sigh as he pulled her in for a hug.

"How was work?" he asked, kissing the top of her head.

"Good. We've just been finalizing all the details."

"Nate sent over the final designs this afternoon. You've done an amazing job."

"Thank you. Launch day is almost here!"

"I know. I can't believe it."

"Your dream is finally coming true."

"More than one," said Jonas as he dipped Mae back and gave her a kiss.

She giggled. "It smells delicious." She righted herself and took a peek in the pan.

"Garlic noodles and shrimp," said Jonas proudly.

"Mmm. My favorite."

Her stomach grumbled loudly again. She clutched her stomach, embarrassed.

"Sounds like someone is hungry," said Jonas with a laugh. He came up behind her and gave the noodles a stir as she leaned back into him. She closed her eyes and breathed him in. She waited a nervous minute as he continued to cook around her.

"I should be…since I'm eating for two."

She watched as Jonas's hand stilled on the spoon. He whirled around and looked at her eyes intently.

"Mae…are you saying you're…"

"Pregnant." She nodded as a smile crept to her lips.

All of a sudden, Jonas let out a loud laugh and he lifted her up onto the counter so she was facing him. He pressed his forehead against hers and shakily lifted his hands to her stomach. She wasn't showing yet. She was just a few weeks along, but he gently laid his hands against her.

"We're having a baby." His eyes were wet with tears.

"Mhmm." She nodded.

Jonas knelt down and excitedly gave her quick kisses all over her face. She threw her head back and laughed.

"We're having a baby!" he shouted this time.

Mae watched as he did a happy dance in the middle of the kitchen. She took a mental snapshot as happiness washed over her. After everything, they were having their happy ending. But it wasn't an ending at all. It was just the beginning.

This is the end of Jonas and Mae's love story.

Want to be notified when the next book in the series featuring Kenny is released?

Or would you like to read a free romance novel from me instead?

For both, click here and subscribe:
https://dl.bookfunnel.com/oe2w1m9zxx

Printed in Great Britain
by Amazon

39421841R00158